KILLED ON THE ICE

KILLED
ON THE ICE

William L. DeAndrea

PUBLISHED FOR THE CRIME CLUB BY

DOUBLEDAY & COMPANY, INC.

GARDEN CITY, NEW YORK

1984

All of the characters in this book
are fictitious, and any resemblance
to actual persons, living or dead,
is purely coincidental.

Library of Congress Cataloging in Publication Data
DeAndrea, William L.
    Killed on the ice. (Crime club)
    I. Title.   II. Series.
PS3554.E174K54   1984   813'.54
ISBN 0-385-18276-7
Library of Congress Catalog Card Number: 83–20673

*For Orania**

*See epigraph, Chapter Ten

KILLED ON THE ICE

"Now's the time to head for something really special . . ."
—Gene Barry, Miller Beer commercial

CHAPTER ONE

It was a scene to give new meaning to the phrase "murdered in cold blood."

The body of Dr. Paul Dinkover lay at the far side of the skating rink, at the end of a long smear of red that was already turning sticky from contact with the ice. I knew that because I bent over to touch it, exactly as if I knew how to judge from the condition of blood how long a man has been dead.

I made a face at myself, looked around for a place to wipe my fingers. I made a mental note to start carrying a handkerchief. I was in mild trouble at the moment, but every second I delayed calling the police made it harsher. In other circumstances I might be able to excuse myself by saying I went to see if I could aid the victim, but that wouldn't work in this case. The cops would know that *I* would know that anybody who'd lost that much blood, anybody who'd had his abdomen as thoroughly ventilated as Dr. Dinkover had, was way beyond aid.

I didn't care. From where the blood started to where the body lay was a good seventy-five feet, maybe more. I had to find out if I could believe my eyes. I had to find out if this old man, in his death agony, had spent his last ounce of energy doing what it seemed he had done.

I started across the ice. I walked in a wide curve, to avoid messing with the blood smear and any evidence the police might be able to read from it. No sense getting in more trouble than necessary.

It's not easy to walk on ice in street shoes. You have to walk slowly, and put your feet down flat with each step. You have to concentrate, but I couldn't put my whole mind to the process. I was thinking about the body, and about the blood drying like rust-colored paint on my fingers.

My concentration was impaired even more when my beeper went off. Some efficiency-mad clown in Accounting had decided that the Network wasn't getting enough mileage out of its executives, so for more than three weeks now, since the beginning of December, I'd had to carry the damn thing, which went off any time somebody decided he couldn't live without Matt Cobb. This probably set a record for inopportune moments. The noise wasn't loud, or even unpleasant, but it was a surprise, and it made me jump. I don't need to jump when I'm trying to walk across a Teflon-smooth sheet of ice. I don't need to be surprised in the company of a corpse.

I regained my balance, unclipped the beeper from my belt, and told it to shut up, which it failed to do. I thrust it deep in the pocket of my overcoat, but it still gave rapid muffled peeps, like a baby bird being smothered. I clenched my teeth and tried to ignore it.

I finally made it to where the body was and looked at the scene. Dr. Dinkover lay half on his side, clutching a piece of cloth to his body. Blood had soaked the cloth, making most of it a uniform red, but a blue corner and two white stars remained to tell me it was supposed to be an American flag. Dinkover had crawled all that way, almost certainly hastening his death, in order to pull over an American flag and bleed on it. His left hand was still bunched in the cloth held tight to his heart; his right was closed over the gold eagle at the top of the flagpole. The heavy metal base of the flagpole had rolled off the little strip of carpet it had been placed on when the set was built and had gouged a deep half-circle in the ice.

I noted all this and filed it (the police were sure to ask questions, and not too politely either), but my mind was still taken up with that last journey of Dr. Dinkover. Dying, he'd grabbed for the American flag. Amazing. In fact, considering his history, damn near incredible.

It was 1:59 A.M. I was inside a light green warehouse sort of a building rather grandly called the Blades Club ("Manhattan's Finest Year-Round Ice Skating Center"). It certainly was a lot finer than the neighborhood. The Blades Club huddled among a whole bunch of buildings that really *were* warehouses, and at this time of night the area got pretty spooky. Even without corpses.

The Network had picked the Blades Club for taping part of "Wendy Ichimi's Springtime Christmas" for several reasons. For one thing, it really was a good sheet of ice; for another, it was only a few blocks west of Madison Square Garden, where Wendy was starring in America's Ice-Travaganza through Christmas Eve. Highlights of her final performance there would also be part of the special, and the Network's logistical people figured that they could tie up less of their new experimental equipment if they moved it from the Blades Club to the Garden when the Olympic Fantasy segment (which Wendy had just finished taping that afternoon) was over with. It would be cheaper than committing a double complement of equipment, and easy, too, because of the distance.

They probably hadn't considered the Blades Club for ease of body disposal, but Manhattan's Finest Year-Round Ice Skating Center could offer that, too. About a hundred yards farther west was the Hudson River; a little way to the north was a huge hole in the ground that would someday become the new convention center.

As I looked at the body again, I have to admit I was tempted. Even if I hadn't been the one to find the body, it was all too evident that the late Dr. Paul Dinkover was going to be my problem, the kind of problem Special Projects is designed to handle.

"Special" in this context means "stuff nobody wants to talk about," as in "special education," or that great standby of TV commercials, "a woman's *special* needs." Well, the Network has special needs, too. Keeping regulating agencies happy. Avoiding scandals. Getting an edge on the competition. I'm in charge of the department that's supposed to handle all that. Mostly we succeed. They call me, but don't treat me like, a vice-president at the Network. I try to keep the department as virtuous as possible, but my definition of virtue is necessarily flexible.

I thought it over and decided I really couldn't stretch it far enough to include getting rid of the body. Ordinarily, it wouldn't have crossed my mind even as a wishful thought, but this was so damned *unfair*. Dr. Dinkover wasn't supposed to be here. He had nothing to do with the Network. He was an old friend of Wendy's father, but he hadn't been invited to the rehearsal. I had, in fact, heard Wendy specifically *dis-*invite him that very afternoon.

But there he was. Uninvited, unexpected, unwelcome, and messily dead. And Matt Cobb's responsibility.

I'd looked at him too long—my stomach began doing calisthenics in an effort to tell me to get out of there. I kept looking for a few more seconds, telling my stomach we'd see who was boss, and to my chagrin almost found out. I started the slow walk back across the ice toward the exit. All the way, I kept seeing the bloody flag clutched to the old man's body. And wondering.

I was just reaching for the handle when the door opened to reveal a seamy-faced guy in an immaculate green coverall with a shiny silk patch on one sleeve that said Blades on it. His name was Gertz, and he was the night attendant.

He was impatient. "It's five past two, mister. They tell me out there you're all done for the night, that's fine with me, but I'm supposed to put the lights out at two o'clock, or you TV guys are stuck for another hour. Golden time, you know?"

I smiled ruefully. Three days' exposure to TV technicians, and he was beginning to talk like one already. "Golden time" is the end of the rainbow for Network employees, and it explains why technicians never get upset if things go wrong. They get time and a half past eight hours, double time past ten, and two and a half times their normal pay for every hour or part thereof after twelve. Golden time.

"So what are you gonna do, mister?" Gertz demanded. "I mean, technically, I shouldn't be giving you no choice at all, but since everybody else is already out of here—"

"How long does it take you to get the lights back on once you turn them off?" I asked.

"Half hour, forty-five minutes. We got these special athletic lights—"

"I know. Leave them on."

"You want me to leave them on?"

"Mmm-hmmm. The police are going to need them, and they won't like waiting for you to get them cranked up again."

"Police? What police?"

"The homicide police." I hooked a thumb back over my shoulder.

Gertz looked. His eyes got wide, and his jaw started to work. I grabbed him by the shoulders and turned him around before his stomach showed him who was boss.

"Leave them on," I said again, leading him from the rink and back to where (I hoped) the Wendy Ichimi party would be waiting.

"Yeah," Gertz said. He was a little better in the corridor, out of sight of the body. His mind went back to first concerns. "I'll leave them on. Only thing is, the owners are real sticklers about this place. Who do I bill this all to?"

"Don't worry," I told him, "somebody will pay for it."

"Now let's meet today's contestants."
—Art Fleming, *Jeopardy* (NBC)

CHAPTER TWO

"What the hell was the flag doing there?" said Detective Lieutenant Cornelius U. Martin, Jr. "That's what I'd like to know." His dark brown face tightened in a scowl. "No. What I'd really like to know is why I always get these damned TV cases."

"I asked for you when I called Headquarters. Luckily, you happened to be on duty tonight."

"Luckily for who?" Lieutenant Martin has known me all my life; his son and I played basketball together. He knows I was an English major in college, and he knows I'll never have the guts to correct him when he says "who" when it should be "whom." That's why he does it.

"Luckily for justice, Mr. M. I think this case is going to call for a lot of understanding between the Network and the police."

"You can save that bullshit, Matty. You and your Network won't get any favoritism from me."

"I didn't ask for favoritism, I asked for understanding."

He grunted. "Tell me about the flag," he said.

"It's supposed to remind you of the Olympics."

"What Olympics? Munich?"

"This is a set for part of a special for Wendy Ichimi. Sort of a flashback fantasy kind of thing. Her world championships. Her gold medal."

"Yeah, I saw her outside. Cute little thing, isn't she?" The lieutenant smiled in spite of himself. Wendy had that effect on people.

"Cute enough to get the Network to fork over a bundle to sign her to do a special."

"Which explains what you're doing here, I suppose. Looking after the Network's bundle."

"Sort of. Dr. Dinkover's been hounding Wendy, trying to get her to do something for one of his causes, and her agent asked us for someone to help fend him off."

"Pretty menial work for a vice-president."

"When there's no crisis going on, all Special Projects work is menial. Besides, I'm only here because I got a frantic call from Max Brother—"

"Who's that?"

"Wendy's agent. I got a call from him. I was going to bed and my beeper went off. Did you ever have to wear one of these things?"

"No. Get on with it."

"I got a call from Max Brother that Brophy hadn't shown up, that he and Wendy had had to come to this disgusting neighborhood in a cab, that if the Network was going to be so cavalier in its commitments, he would just hire somebody tomorrow from a top agency and bill the Network for it. He said—"

"Wait a minute," the lieutenant said. "Brophy didn't show up?"

"That's right."

"Harris Brophy? The one who works for you?"

"That's the one, and before you say anything, I don't believe it either. There are a lot of things wrong with Harris, but irresponsibility isn't one of them. I called the Network to set my overnight man searching for him before I got over here."

"Why didn't you send the overnight man and look for Brophy yourself?"

"I thought of it, but I decided it would take at least a vice-president to mollify an angry agent. I had no idea how the star would be taking it."

"How did she?"

"Turned out she was fine. Said she was worried about Harris."

Lieutenant Martin took off his hat, the one he had owned since before hats came back into fashion, and ran a hand over his white hair. "Jesus," he said, "Brophy missing. I hope *he* doesn't turn up dead somewhere. One of your goddam Network murders at a time is already too much."

"Thank you. I can tell you're really trying to cheer me down."

"Don't mention it." He looked at me suspiciously. "Matty, no crap now. Can you tell me one single solitary thing more that will be of any help at all? I mean, I am gonna get pressure put on me (thanks to you) about this thing from just about *everybody*."

I knew what he meant. Paul Dinkover was famous in a lot of ways. He had first come to prominence in the late forties. He was perhaps the most renowned American psychiatrist alive by the mid-fifties. He'd been a devout Jungian at first, but he had theories that grew into heresies as far as Dr. Jung and the faithful were concerned. Soon Dinkover had become a psychiatric movement in himself.

He became more than renowned about 1960 when he collaborated with a twenty-five-year-old journalist named Carla Nelson on two books that served to popularize his theories. *Sex in a Sane Society* sold an astronomical number of copies; *Signs, Symbols, and Sanity* sold in numbers that were only slightly less incredible. The titles probably accounted for the difference. In any case, they made Dinkover rich, and they continued to do so. Even today, nobody in any college anywhere takes an introductory psych course without reading at least one of these books, probably both.

In 1961 Dinkover went from fame to notoriety when the fifty-year-old psychiatrist was hit with a very messy divorce suit by his wife of twenty-eight years, who named several women, including Carla Nelson, as corespondents. Soon after the divorce was granted, Dinkover married Miss Nelson, which was good for a few more headlines.

But the amazing Dr. Dinkover got his biggest, loudest headlines during the late sixties and early seventies, after he had retired from his practice altogether. He became a very visible leader of the anti-Vietnam war movement. His position (he said) was based on the proposition that he had wasted his life trying to help people to sanity in the midst of a society that could perpetrate insanities like genocide and Nixon. (He always could turn a phrase, no matter what you think of the sentiment.) He was especially visible during the murder and terrorism trial of the Landover Four, heading the drive to raise money for their defense, and acting as media spokesman for them during the trial. We still have the tapes in the Network library—he got a lot of publicity for the four, but he didn't do them much good. He did, however, turn a few spiffy phrases when the four were convicted. Eric Sevareid on CBS called it the best piece of oratory to come from the Vietnam protest movement.

After 1975, when the war came to its ignominious end, and the boys (including me) came home, Dr. Dinkover seemed to be at a loss for a cause titanic enough to match his energies. He turned up here and there, using one cause or another as a forum to tell Americans how corrupt and crazy they all were, but the parade had more or less passed him by.

Still, Lieutenant Martin's point was well taken. Dinkover had been good copy for more than thirty years, and his death by violence at age eighty-two, added to the fact that he had apparently used his own death as an opportunity to take one last swipe at American society, was going to make the investigation into a combination pressure cooker and a circus.

"I'm sorry," I told him sadly. "There's nothing. The Network is only involved in this by accident. I happened to be here."

Lieutenant Martin sighed. "All right, dammit. Let's see what I can learn from the others."

They were sitting impatiently on the slippery bus-station plastic chairs that filled the waiting room of the Blades Club. Five of them, all part of Wendy's entourage—no Network personnel. The Olympic Fantasy segment had already been taped and the equipment moved, but the Network had reserved the rink to give Wendy a place to practice her special routine for the Christmas Eve show.

I got a wry nod from Detective First Grade Horace A. Rivetz. Rivetz was a tough, wiry little guy who was wry about everything. His typical response to any tale of human depravity was, "It figures."

I nodded back, and took a seat with my fellow suspects. Rivetz introduced us, pointing at each of us in turn, even though I've told him repeatedly it's impolite. "Max Brother, agent. Ivan Danov, coach. Wendy Ichimi—she's the star of this mess . . ." I couldn't tell if he meant the show or the murder. "Mrs. Harry Speir, Miss Ichimi's *step-mother* . . ."

Rivetz came down heavy on the step, though it didn't take a degree in ethnology to realize that small, light brown Wendy, with her delicate Oriental features, had no actual blood relationship to big, pink, corn-fed Helena Speir. Mrs. Speir was white-haired and handsome, and she had strong gray eyes that she kept turning toward her stepdaughter. Her look was unadulterated motherly concern, blood or no blood.

". . . Beatrice Dunney, another skater in the show . . ." Bea Dunney was a blonde, six inches taller than Wendy and probably thirty pounds heavier, but somehow she seemed a lot more vulnerable at the moment. It was probably fatigue—she was probably pretty under most circumstances, but now her blue eyes were puffy and bloodshot, and her fair skin was blotched with red. The expression she wore, an embarrassed I'm-only-here-by-accident-don't-mind-me half-smile, didn't help. I knew from experience that cops tend to get peeved by that attitude, and it didn't improve her looks much either.

Her expression only wavered for a second, when Rivetz referred to her as "another skater." Then her mouth got tight and rueful, and her eyes flashed something that wasn't joy.

". . . and Cobb you know," Rivetz concluded.

The lieutenant grunted. "Thanks. All right, ladies and gentlemen. I'm Detective Lieutenant Martin, and I'll be investigating this case. Does everyone know what happened here tonight?"

There were nods. Ivan Danov grumbled something that sounded like "Of course."

"All right," the lieutenant said again, "then the first thing I want to know is—"

Wendy Ichimi spoke for the first time in my presence since I'd found the body. "What *I* want to know is what he was even *doing* here!" She tossed her head, making the highlights dance in her shiny black hair.

That was another part of Wendy's appeal. Her big almond eyes and tiny turned-up nose and her mouth, which was small and round and made her look as if she were in a perpetual state of surprise, were beautiful and exotic and spoke of the Mysterious East. At the same time, her voice and gestures and attitudes were pure California Girl. It was an intriguing combination.

"Now, Wendy," Max Brother said. He was undoubtedly the handsomest man in the building. With his expensively styled hair and his sleepy dark eyes, he looked like a silent movie star. He was probably fifteen years older than he looked, which would make him fifty. His well-publicized bout with cocaine hadn't left a mark on him. Brother was this era's super agent. They come along every once in a while, short but handsome guys from New York who break into the business as singers or comics or chorus boys and hang on for a while because what they lack in talent, they make up in drive. Eventually, they realize that drive itself is a pretty valuable commodity, and they start using it on behalf of someone who has talent. Anybody. Brother's specialty was girl nightclub singers and rock groups. Wendy was his first athlete, but he wasn't doing badly by her at all, if the contract he'd gotten out of the Network was any indication.

"Now *what*, Max?" Wendy demanded. "All I want to know is how that slimy old bastard got *in* here when I told him this afternoon I never wanted to see him again!"

"Oh, Wendy," her stepmother said, chagrined by either the language or the sentiment, I couldn't tell which.

Max Brother smiled at Wendy, but there was anger in his eyes. "I just think we should let the lieutenant and his men do their job." It came out "theya jawb." Max had conquered his New York accent for the most part, but apparently it would sneak back in times of stress. "I'm sure they're better at asking questions about this sort of thing than we are."

He shot the lieutenant a quick grin that was intended to include him in the Society for Getting Silly Young Girls to Butt Out, but Mr. M. wasn't interested.

"I don't think Miss Ichimi is doing so bad for a beginner. Let's try to get her question answered. Who *did* let Dr. Dinkover in here tonight?"

Silence.

The lieutenant let it go on for a long time, looking at each of us in turn. I was slightly put out at being included in his dirty look since I'd already told him *I* didn't let Dinkover into the Blades Club, but I figured he just wanted to make things fair.

The silence went on. Finally, the lieutenant said, "Look. This Dr. Dinkover was famous for a lot of things, but picking locks wasn't among them. So somebody let him in. I'm going to find out who. Now the easy way is if you tell me. The hard way is unpleasant for everybody, especially for the one who let him in, because when I have to do things the hard way, I get angry.

"Now, I'm going to ask one more time, without prejudice as the lawyers say."

"Lawyers!" Ivan Danov exploded. In the few days I'd known him, I'd come to learn that he literally never spoke except in explosions, as if he had to let the words pile up in him to a critical mass before they could force themselves past the barrier of a foreign language.

"Lawyers!" he said again. "Why do we not have lawyers? Why have we not heard our rights? I demand my rights. I demand the rights of my friends. I demand the rights of my students. I demand them in the name of Democracy! Why do you think, in my old age, I have defected from Russia? For Freedom! I would think you, a black man, would have the knowledge of what oppression means—"

The lieutenant did a little exploding himself. *"Quiet!"* Danov shut up but only to gather air for a new explosion. "Look, Mr. Danov, this is a *field investigation.* Nobody's been arrested. Nobody's been singled out as a suspect. That's a popular misconception. If you are innocent, it's your duty to assist in the investigation. Did you let him in? Do you know who did?"

Danov was a tall, lanky man with sparse silver hair. He had won three gold medals for Russia during the fifties and sixties, then retired to coaching. All had been fine until Soviet athletic authorities decided that Danov's most promising pupil, who happened to be a Jew, was not quite right and for his own good had to be sent off to one of Russia's famous "sanitariums" until he was cured, or until it rained up instead of down, whichever came last.

Danov had never been interested in politics, but he knew skating, and knew he was the best. He defected to the United States in protest, he had told the press, "of this crime against Sport, of this crime against Danov!"

"First I will hear my rights!" he insisted.

Lieutenant Martin sighed. "All right, Rivetz, read him his rights."

Rivetz was very good at dirty looks, and he used an especially potent one on Danov as he recited the Miranda Warnings, but it was all wasted. The skating coach spent the time nodding at the rest of us, satisfied in the knowledge that he had struck a blow for Freedom.

Rivetz got to the end of his little spiel, asking Danov if he understood all of it. Danov said of course. The lieutenant asked again if Danov had let the victim in.

"No," Danov said.

The lieutenant scraped his upper lip against his lower teeth. "Why didn't you just say so? You weren't about to incriminate yourself with that statement."

"Right is right," Danov said.

"It sure is. Right is definitely right." The lieutenant gave me another dirty look, as though I were personally responsible for his troubles. I shrugged.

"Okay," Lieutenant Martin said. "You've all given statements to the detectives—we'll be asking you to sign them sometime tomorrow when we get them all typed up for you. If you need to leave town any time soon, check with us first, all right?"

Max Brother was about to get huffy, then thought better of it.

Lieutenant Martin said, "Cobb, I know these are busy people. When I want to speak to any of them, I'll work through you."

I nodded.

"All right then. You can go ho—"

The lieutenant was being nice, or at least circumspect. He could have kept us a lot longer and been a lot rougher on us, and he probably would have if it weren't for the fame and money of the victim and the suspects. Still, there we were, one phoneme from being dismissed, when Wendy's stepmother opened her mouth.

"Lieutenant," she said. "Lieutenant, I was just thinking . . ."

"Yes, ma'am?"

"Well, I was just thinking, how did Mr. *Cobb* get in here tonight?"

That got me a whole lot of dirty looks.

"Drizzle, drazzle, drozzle, drome,
Time for this one to go home."
—Sandy Becker, *Tutor the*
Turtle (syndicated)

CHAPTER THREE

"I mean," Helena Speir went on, "here we are, puzzling over how Paul got inside—"

My turn to interrupt. "Paul?"

In spite of everything, Wendy smiled. Mrs. Speir ignored me.

"—but Mr. Cobb arrived only when we were about ready to go, after Wendy and Beatrice had finished and were off the ice, and how did he get in? The caretaker couldn't have—I saw him go into his office."

She paused for breath. "I don't mean to imply anything," she said, implying plenty, "but if there was no difficulty for Mr. Cobb to get in, there shouldn't have been any for Paul."

"Thank you, Mrs. Speir, but Cobb's entry has already been accounted for."

Mrs. Speir started to get a little red. "Well, I was just trying to help."

"Mr. M., mind if I explain? I still have to work with these people." He nodded. "I have a key," I told them. I pointed at Rivetz, who held up a plastic thing that looked like a credit card. "A magnetic strip thing. Since there's only one attendant here late at night, and he's got a lot to do, the rink gives out keys to regular members who are planning to use the facilities at those times. When we made the deal to use the place for Miss Ichimi's special, they gave the Network a few of them."

Now Mrs. Speir got very red. "Oh, Mr. Cobb, I'm sorry. I really didn't mean to imply . . . It's not likely Paul had one of these, is it?"

"Not unless he belonged to the club," I said. But it got me thinking. I'd kept one of the Network keys; Ed Argiulo, who was directing Wendy's show, had another; and the third had been given to Harris Brophy. And Harris was missing.

The lieutenant sighed again, his biggest one of the night, and this time he did manage to let us go home. Or, rather, he let us go. It was pushing 3:30 A.M., but I had a lot to do before I could go home.

The first thing I had to do was see the ladies back to their hotel; they were staying at the Statler, which is right across the street from Madison Square Garden. Max Brother, it seemed, was going directly to his office in order to be able to deal with the press. Danov was staying with friends in the city. Lieutenant Martin had me escorted to a phone to call for a couple of cabs. It would be impossible to hail one on the street in that neighborhood at that time of night.

As soon as we got settled in the cab, Helena Speir apologized again for, as she put it, "embarrassing me."

I told her not to mention it. "From the way you spoke of him, I gather you knew Dr. Dinkover."

"Yes, Paul was a close friend of Henry's—Wendy's father—at the University."

I knew Wendy's father had been a hotshot mathematician, but this was the first I'd heard of any connection between him and Dinkover. I was trying to think of an inoffensive way to follow this up, but Wendy interrupted.

"Anybody have a cigarette?" she asked.

In my work I meet a lot of people whose entire livelihood depends on their ability to breathe and/or speak properly. Singers. Disc jockeys. Actors. Athletes. Dancers. I'm no longer surprised at the number of these people who smoke. Appalled, yes, but not surprised.

Bea Dunney dug a pack out of her purse and gave it to Wendy. The champion lit it, took a drag, looked at me with a wicked smile, and said, "You won't tell on me, will you, Mr. Cobb? I have to maintain a positive image for all the little skaters out there. And to the moms and dads who pay to take them to the ice shows."

I told her her secret was safe with me. She said good, then turned and leaned her forehead against the window as if the rest of us didn't exist.

The cab made a U-turn on Broadway, something that is possible only very late at night, and stopped in front of the hotel. I paid and tipped the driver on behalf of the Network.

I ushered the ladies inside and walked them to the elevator. They kept assuring me I didn't have to go to all that trouble, but I told them I had wanted to come inside to make a phone call. Mrs. Speir said I could make the call from the suite she and Wendy shared, and I took her up on it. I had been hoping she'd make the offer. It wasn't that the Network was too cheap to spend a dime on a phone call; it was the fact that I had already found one messy corpse this morning, and it was stimulating my imagination. I had visions of a bloody-handed fiend waiting behind the door of Wendy's room, and I didn't like them.

I also figured it would be an opportunity for me to fill in the blanks about Dinkover's background as it concerned Wendy's late father.

I was wrong about that part of it. We dropped Bea Dunney at her floor, and I watched unobtrusively until she was safely into her room before I let the doors close. Then we proceeded upstairs, where I made sure Wendy and her mother would be safe. I always feel a little foolish when it turns out I've been worrying over nothing, but I feel a *lot* foolish on those occasions when it turns out I've failed to worry over *something*.

Then I made my phone call. I had remembered (at last) about the Network's trying to beep me all those years ago while I had been crossing the ice toward Dinkover's body.

"Special Projects, St. John," said a voice.

"Al?" I said, "Matt Cobb. Listen, we've got a—"

"Matt?" St. John said. "Where have you *been?* Shirley must have beeped you twelve times before she left, and I tried a few times myself before I gave up."

"My beeper was in my coat, and my coat was in another room."

"Good Lord, Matt," he said. Al St. John was a blond Ivy League type who'd joined the Network about the same time I became head of Special Projects. He was full of questions about the TV business, and suggestions about how we could improve operations in the department. He was very smart—he was about three inches from a Ph.D. in psychology—but I always had a hard time forgetting he wasn't a kid dressed up. It wasn't only the way he looked, it was the way he talked.

All his expletives were out of boys' literature. "Good Lord" was about as irreverent as he got. That and "Judas Priest." I had never actually heard him say "Great Scott" or "Holy Smoke," but I figured it was just a matter of time.

"Good Lord, Matt," he said again. "If you don't keep the beeper with you, it can't do any good." I think he got off on having a beeper.

"*Mea culpa,*" I said. "Now, where did Shirley go?" I wanted to know the answer, all right, but I was dreading it just the same. Shirley Arnstein was a former congressional staffer, plain in a pleasant sort of way, and very shy, except when it came to her work. She was devoted to the Network with an almost religious zeal. She was the only person I never had to apologize to for assigning her for a week of overnight duty. She loved it. If she were the only one there, she wouldn't have to worry about sharing any of the work. It would have to have been something drastic to make her walk out in the middle of a shift.

"She's at the hospital, Matt."

"What happened to her?"

"Not her, Harris. The last I heard from Shirley, he was still unconscious. Or rather unconscious again. He came to long enough at one point to tell the people in the emergency room he'd been mugged and to call the Network. Shirley was working the graveyard shift so she heard the news first. She tried to get you—"

"I was busy."

"—but you didn't answer. So she beeped me. I'm surprised she waited for me to get here before she left. You know how she feels about Harris."

I nodded, realized that was stupid over the phone, and said, "Yes." Shirley Arnstein's devotion to duty was equaled only by her devotion to Harris Brophy, a fact Harris only noticed when he had nothing else on the agenda. It was not the healthiest of situations, and I'd often thought that someday it was going to cause me trouble. I remember thinking this could be it, if Shirley went off the rails over it.

I got the address of the hospital from Al and told him to hold the fort until further notice. Then I gave him a quick briefing on the evening's other disaster.

"Good Lord," he said. "It's hitting the fan from both directions, isn't it? What do I tell the press, Matt?"

The press, for God's sake. "You tell them *nothing.* Come on, Al, you know better than that. This is just a terrible coincidence, Dinkover had nothing to do with the Network; the police will tell them anything they want to know."

"I figured that would be it. Never hurts to make sure."

I rubbed my eyes. "You're right, Al, I'm just tired. I'll get back to you as soon as I can."

"Wear your beeper," he said.

In spite of fatigue and everything else, I had to smile. "You got it."

After I hung up, Wendy, who had been pretending not to listen, asked me if everything was okay.

"No," I said.

"Was that about Harris? Mr. Brophy?"

"Yes. Apparently, someone has beaten him up pretty badly."

"I'm sorry to hear it. He was nice."

"I'm on my way to the hospital now. I'll tell him you said so, if he's up to hearing it."

She didn't say anything else, so I figured it was okay to go. I was almost out the door when I heard her voice behind me. "Mr. Cobb?" I turned to look at her.

"I want to talk to you. Tomorrow sometime, okay? The ice show matinee is over a little past three. Can you meet me at the Garden."

"I don't know yet. I'll try."

"Thank you. And, Mr. Cobb?" I stopped again. "No matter what you think from the way I acted tonight, I'm not really a bitch."

I told her I'd take her word for it and left.

CHAPTER FOUR

I'd never seen Shirley Arnstein like this before. Her eyes were red from crying. When she saw me, she forgot her usual shyness, ran to me, held me, and started to irrigate my shoulder.

That's supposed to be a pleasant sensation for a man, and to let you in on a little secret, it usually is, *but only if you have some idea of what the hell you're supposed to do to make things better.*

In this case, when I still wasn't one hundred percent sure what the problem was yet, it was more than a little uncomfortable. I gave Shirley an avuncular pat on the back and made noises that were the functional equivalent of "there, there."

Then I spoiled everything by asking how Harris was.

Shirley pulled away as if I'd hit her, and for the first time, I thought oh God, he's dead.

With an effort it was painful to watch, Shirley Arnstein caught herself on the brink of hysterics. I stood there looking at her for what must have been a half minute while she took deep breaths with her eyes closed. She was pressing her knuckles into her temples, hard, as if she wanted to keep her head from coming apart. I wished she'd stop.

Finally, she did. In a clear, perfectly normal voice, she said, "They're operating on him, Matt. They have to relieve the pressure on his spine. Something like that. Or he may wind up paralyzed. He might anyway. Or he might even die."

Shirley's face had already died. It looked white and waxy, like the little bottles they used to sell cheap syrup drinks in.

"He's not going to die," I said.

"I want to believe that."

"He's too ornery." Shirley didn't say anything, but she shook her head and looked sad. She thinks Harris is badly misunderstood by everybody but her.

I spent the next forty minutes or so tracking down Harris's belongings. The operating room people sent me to the emergency room, who sent me to the admitting office, who sent me back to the emergency room, who sent me to security, who, to the salvation of what remained of my sanity, turned out to have the stuff. They'd kept it because the police were sending someone from the lab to pick it up. The plan, I suppose, was to vacuum it and see if they could pull something out of it that would help identify the attacker. I got a look at it, and from what I could see, all they were likely to vacuum out of Harris's clothes was a lot of dried blood.

That was all I could tell from five feet. The head of security, a mustached giant with a nasty-looking .357 magnum on his belt and a nameplate on his chest that read Cernak, wouldn't let me get any closer.

"Anybody touches that stuff," he explained, "it's my ass." He prodded the point home with a finger the size of a hammer handle. I was sure I'd go home later and find little oval bruises on my chest.

I explained to Cernak that I certainly didn't want it to be his ass, but that I was aflame with curiosity about my friend's belongings.

"How about letting me look a little closer, Cernak, that's all I ask. There's one specific thing I want to see."

"No way, man." He had large, very sensitive brown eyes. Dedicated. Unyielding.

"Cernak," I said. It never occurred to me to call him Mr. Cernak or to find out what his first name was. The name suited him, as if he were the title character in a barbarian movie—*Cernak! Son of the Fire God.* That kind of thing.

"Cernak," I said again. "I understand you're doing your job, and I won't bother you any more about touching or looking at Mr. Brophy's things."

"That's good." He looked down at me. I'm no shrimp, but Cernak looked down at me a long way. "I'm glad to hear it. You were beginning to bug me."

"Will you answer a couple of questions for me?"

He took off his cap and brushed a few errant black curls back into place. "I might have been a lot more willing to do that if you didn't come on so strong in the first place . . ."

I recognized the tone in his voice that said he was leading up to a deal. It's a sad fact of life that to do the work of the Department of Special Projects, I have to cross a lot of palms with Network silver, but I had never figured the honest-eyed Cernak as a bribe seeker. I had mixed emotions. I was glad to see I had a chance to make some progress, which had been damned scarce tonight, but I was disappointed in Cernak.

"The thing is," he went on, "if I answer the wrong kind of question, it's my ass."

I was very tired. "If it's your ass, don't answer, all right?"

Cernak shrugged massively. He did everything massively. "Okay, ask away, but afterwards, you gotta do something for me."

"Of course," I said. "The first thing I want to know is who undressed the patient?"

"Emergency room orderlies. Routine mugging, you know how that goes. Cops and me watched them; the cops like a witness when a patient says something, and this guy was starting to babble about that time, so they had me sit in. None of these emergency room orderlies speaks English too good. Not many of the doctors, either, come to that. Also, they didn't undress him, exactly. 'Cause of his head. They cut the clothes off of him."

I took another glimpse at the bloody rags. "Yeah, I could have figured that myself, if I'd thought about it." Still, I was running in luck. Cernak had seen Harris brought in; he could tell me of his own knowledge what I wanted to know.

"What did he have in his pockets?"

Cernak looked at me.

"What did he have in his pockets?" I asked again.

"What do you think?"

"I think, goddammit, that as big as you are, I'm going to take a swing at your nose in about five seconds."

He laughed at me. I'm six feet two inches tall and close to the condition I was in when I played basketball. I'm not used to being laughed at when I suggest I'm going to take some sort of physical action, but the Son of the Fire God laughed, and I wasn't even surprised.

"Come on, man," he said, still laughing. "I *said* it was a routine mugging. A little more vicious than usual, maybe, but routine. They don't leave *anything* behind in somebody's pockets but lint, know what I mean?"

I knew what he meant, but I wanted to make sure. "No wallet?" I said. "No keys? No credit cards?" The key to the Blades Club looked like a credit card.

"Nope. If he had a wad of Kleenex to blow his nose, they got that, too. Satisfied?" I nodded. "Good," Cernak said. "Now you got to do something for me."

I started to reach for my wallet, but the Son of the Fire God renewed my faith in human nature. He confused me, first, though.

"You work for the Network, right? I want you to tell me if Cathy is going to marry that son-of-a-bitch Atherton."

I said something intelligent, like "Huh?"

"On *Agony of Love*, man. The soap opera. I work on the night shift, so the soaps are my favorite shows. Let me tell you, Cathy is driving me *crazy*. She's way too good for that bastard. If I was her . . ."

I told him what he wanted to know. He shook my hand and thanked me profusely. I got back upstairs just in time to hear a doctor tell Shirley that Harris was going to live, but that we'd just have to wait to find out what, if any, permanent damage had been done. The attack had been very methodical. Three blows with a pipe or something similar, all delivered to strategic areas (head, ribs, and knee), all designed to leave Harris incapacitated for a long period. The doctor said that if a concerned passerby hadn't called an ambulance as soon as he had, Harris would be dead. Now the doctor thought he was going to be all right.

Shirley started to cry again, happy tears this time. I let her cry while I dealt with a functionary who wanted to know if Harris had Blue Cross.

The next thing on the agenda was a trip to Harris's apartment. I had

to decide whether to take Shirley with me. It might be a bit much for
her to take; on the other hand, getting back to work, especially on
something that hit her hard and personally, might be just what she
needed.

"Shirley," I said, "we've got work to do."

"Wh—what, Matt?"

"Harris's place. The mugger got his wallet and his keys—that means
he knows where Harris lives and had the means to get in."

"Oh, God, you're right! Let's go, maybe he's still there." That
proved Shirley was taking this personally—ordinarily she'd suggest we
go by the book and ask the police to check it out. This time, her voice
and expression promised a nasty experience for the mugger if we found
him in.

Not that it was likely, of course—hours had passed, and any thief
who had intended to follow up his assault on Harris Brophy's person
with one on his possessions was long gone by now.

Shirley had grabbed a Network car to come to the hospital, one of
our fleet of luxurious but totally impractical black-on-the-outside,
white-on-the-inside land yachts. We crossed the parking lot just in time
for me to chase a budding young car thief away from it (that's one of
the reasons they're impractical—car thieves find them irresistible, and
Special Projects has to waste time chasing about one a month), got
inside, and headed downtown and west to Harris's apartment.

On the way, I asked Shirley if she had a key to the place. She
blushed. I had to keep my eyes on the road, so I got only a glimpse, but
I could feel the heat of it. She practically glowed in the dim interior of
the car.

"Sorry," I said. "I was just wondering if I'd have to bring the super
in on this or what."

"No, Matt, it's okay. I do have one."

"That saves a little trouble."

About ten blocks and half a minute later, Shirley said, "But I've
never used it before," as though there'd been no pause at all. "I—I was
always afraid I'd barge in on him with some other girl. So I stayed
away." She looked at her hands.

"We're here," I said. "Give me the keys." She fumbled in her purse and handed them over. "Which ones are they?" I asked, because Shirley carried more keys with her, it seemed, than Captain Kangaroo.

She sorted out Harris's front-door key and outside key from the rest. Then I asked her which was which.

Shirley looked miserable. "I don't know, I've never used them."

"Okay," I said, "it probably doesn't matter." That was true; it probably wouldn't. The only way it would make a difference would be if Harris's playmate actually were still inside the apartment with a pipe or a monkey wrench or whatever the hell it was he'd rearranged Harris's bones with. In that case, my jingling keys until I sounded like Santa and his reindeer paying an early call would give him plenty of time to prepare a reception for me. Probably not milk and cookies.

The night—or rather the morning (false dawn was already lighting the sky to the east)—was cold and clear. I put my gloves on, but I left my overcoat unbuttoned, for better freedom of movement.

"Shirley, if I make a noise like I'm in trouble, or if I don't come out in five minutes, drive like hell and get all the cops you can find."

"I'm coming in with you," she said. It was the first time in memory she had openly defied an order from the vice-president in charge of Special Projects.

"You are coming in as soon as I find out if it's safe. Don't worry about it, it's probably nothing."

Shirley didn't like it much, but habit won out, and she nodded. I got out of the car.

Harris Brophy had a floor-through apartment in a converted warehouse in the far West Village, a neighborhood bounded by Fourteenth Street on the north, the Hudson River on the west, and Ninth Avenue on the east. It was, by statistics, one of the safest neighborhoods in Manhattan. These were the same kind of statistics that would give a safe-neighborhood rating to the Sea of Tranquility, i.e., statistics that show practically nobody lives there. It was very spooky to be standing on a sidewalk in New York City and see no automobiles, hear no noises but some honking out on the river. I shivered, and not just from the December cold.

I walked up to Harris's building and took a look at the lock. The first thing I realized was that I had been a jerk to put my gloves on, because I had to take them off to work the key. The second thing I realized was

that the brand of key matched up with the brand of lock (both Rabsons
—you work Special Projects, you learn about good locks), so that knowing which one to use to get in would be easy after all.

Taking great care to keep the rest of Shirley's keys from making
noise, I opened the door and stepped in. The hallway was well lit, but
silent. Harris had the second floor. I tiptoed upstairs, walking well to
the wall side. The building was newly renovated, and new stairs aren't
supposed to squeak, but why take chances?

Somewhere in the building a phone was ringing. I froze and listened.
It rang three times, then stopped, answered, no doubt, by an irate
tenant whose first words would be, "Do you know what *time* it is?"

I walked to the door with the discreet peephole with "H. Brophy"
written underneath, put my ear to the door, and listened. Nothing. I
left it there, snuggled up to the metal of the door. Still nothing.

Carefully, like a gentle lover, I eased the key into the lock. I turned it
so slowly, my wrist began to ache. I heard the faint click as the tum-
blers eased back. That was good; a new lock, well oiled. Then, all at
once, I wrenched the knob around and rammed the door with my
shoulder. The door shot open into a blackened room. I didn't waste any
time being a silhouette in the doorway for whoever might be waiting in
the blackness. Instead, I kept low and let my momentum take me into
a sliding dive across the floor.

It was *supposed* to be a sliding dive. I didn't slide too far because of
what I landed on, something that was knobby and sharp and crunched
under me.

My first thought was that it was a booby trap, but after a few seconds
I realized that while I wasn't exactly comfortable, I was at least still
alive. More important, nobody had tried to jump on me and finish me
off.

I sighed. Another precaution that turned out to have been a foolish
one. I got to my feet to the sound of more crunching. Something that
felt like glass sliced into my hand. Maybe I should have kept my gloves
on after all.

I cursed and brought my hand to my mouth, to suck the wound. I
spit out a piece of glass and continued to rise, more carefully this time.
As I did so, my imagination got taken with the notion that *this* was the
booby trap, that the glass that had cut me was from a test tube that had

been stolen just that morning from some secret government laboratory, and it had held plague bacillus that I had even now loosed on the unsuspecting metropolis.

I cursed again and told myself to stop it. I found a light and turned it on.

Chaos. Someone had trashed Harris's apartment but good. Chairs and tables had been overturned, the contents of drawers strewn everywhere. I'd never been there before and had no mental inventory of Harris's belongings, but I would bet at least half of the Network's profits for the year nearly concluded that he had owned a stereo system and a television set. Both were gone.

What I had fallen on and smashed was a Christmas tree, a little Scotch pine that the thief had apparently knocked over in his haste. I saw now that my overcoat was encrusted across the chest with pieces of colored glass from shattered ornaments. They looked like a row of military decorations.

I stood there looking at the tree for a few seconds, then went downstairs to get Shirley.

She took one look at the room and began to cry again.

"Shirley, I'm sorry, but you've been here a lot, right?"

"Y-yes. But I never used the key Harris gave me."

"All right, I'm not saying you did. All I want to know is what's missing."

Give Shirley a job and she does it. Still sniffling occasionally, she turned slowly, giving the place a good once over. "Well, there's the TV and the stereo and the tape machine. And his coin collection."

"Coin collection?"

She pointed to a blank spot on the wall. "Harris has a collection of Indian head pennies. Since he was little. He had it framed, you know? It's worth almost ten thousand dollars, Harris said."

I sucked more blood out of my hand and thought, you learn something new every day. Harris had never struck me as the coin collecting type. He'd never struck me as the Christmas tree type, either, but Shirley explained that next.

"Oh, Matt, he put the tree up for *me*. You know, I get mad at Harris for being so . . . so detached, for being, I don't know, like a transient in his own life, for being contemptuous of anything sentimental or even human . . .

"I was mad at him today, for flirting with that shameless Japanese girl. Right in front of me. Not that I have any claim on him, but damn him, he *knows* how I feel!"

Shirley wasn't even looking at me. She was just saying it to get it said. It had the sound of something she'd been holding onto for a long time.

"He called me," she went on. "Wanted me to come here tonight. Said he had a surprise for me. It must have been the tree."

I thought it figured Harris would put up a Christmas tree as a surprise for a Jewish girl, but at least it was human and sentimental and a step in the right direction.

"He wanted me to come here," Shirley said again, "but I wouldn't. I said I had to work late, but that was just an excuse. I was still mad, that's all. And now, now . . ."

Shirley was close to losing it again, but the ringing of a telephone somewhere in the apartment cut her off.

"Is this the party to whom I am speaking?"
—Lily Tomlin, *Rowan and Martin's Laugh-In*
(NBC)

CHAPTER FIVE

I put my gloves back on before looking for the phone. The police would eventually dust this place for prints. It wouldn't do them any good, but far be it from me to spoil routine. What I did spoil was the gloves themselves, since only too late did I realize I would be making the inside of the left one a bloody, disgusting mess. It's little touches like this that make life so rewarding.

Anyway, the phone was under a pile of Harris's clothes, and I got to it just as it rang the third time.

"Hello?" I said. I kept my voice light, just above a whisper, in case there was something to learn by having the caller think I was Harris.

No such luck. "Matt?" said Al St. John. "I was hoping I'd find you there—I couldn't think of anywhere else to call."

"You gave me a heart attack, Al. I just want you to know that. You didn't do much for Shirley's health, either."

"Is Shirley with you?"

"That was a stupid question, wasn't it? Of *course* she's with me. What's the matter?"

"Some reporter for the *Times* woke up Mr. Falzet and asked him about the murder of Dr. Dinkover."

"Jesus," I said conversationally. "I bet Falzet loved that."

Tom Falzet was the president of the Network, survivor of one of the few corporate power struggles in the history of American business that actually resulted in backstabbing in more than the figurative sense. Falzet was honest and very good at his job, and those are the last good things you're going to hear about him from me. His opinion of me was similar, if not downright congruent, and I suspect he would have fired me long ago if he didn't suspect I would be delighted to have him out of my hair. I know I probably would have quit long ago if I didn't think he would be glad to be rid of me.

None of this was any secret, and Al was sort of tiptoeing around the matter.

". . . anyway, they said you'd left the hospital, and that Shirley had gone too. I figured, good Lord, where would you have gone except to check out Harris's place, so I called you. I'm glad it worked out."

"Me, too. What does Falzet want?"

"He wants to see you in his office. First thing in the morning."

"No."

"Uh . . . Okay, Matt, I'll tell him I couldn't reach you."

I yawned. "Tell him I said no, Al. For God's sake. I've been up all night. What is it now, about a quarter to five?"

"Exactly a quarter to five." I smiled. It's a little talent I have—I always know what time it is within ten minutes or so. Someday, I told myself, I'll figure out a use for it. At the moment, all it was good for was saving me the effort of moving the sleeve of my overcoat to look at my watch.

"All right. First thing in the morning for our esteemed president is about six hours from now. There is no way on God's green earth I'm going to stay up for another six hours just for the pleasure of his company. I'm going to go home, walk the dog, and go to bed. Tell him I'll see him this afternoon. *Late* this afternoon."

"He's having lunch with the senator this afternoon."

"See? I'm so tired, I forgot. This evening, if he wants. Tomorrow. I'll see him when I'm up to dealing with him."

"All right, Matt, I'll handle it."

"Good, do that. By the way, Harris is going to be all right, his doctor says."

"Oh, that's terrific. I'm sorry to admit that with everything that's been going on, I forgot all about him. Did you get a chance to talk to him? Find out who hit him?" Al was being properly concerned, but the truth was, he and Harris didn't get along too well. I think Al resented the fact that Harris was my top man, and would be until he quit.

"No," I said, "they had to operate. Harris was still out when we left. And don't worry about forgetting. Dealing with Falzet is enough to scramble anybody's brain."

"I still shouldn't have forgotten him completely. Tell Shirley I sympathize with her."

"I will. This has been a tough night." I'm a master of understatement. "You've done good work, Al."

He thanked me, a little more warmly than necessary, and we hung up. Shirley said, "Are you going to call the police now?"

"Soon," I said. "Not from here. I've been hung up at the scene of one crime already tonight."

"That was thoughtful of you, telling Al he did a good job," Shirley said. "That sort of thing means a lot."

I shrugged. "Facts are facts."

"A good boss points out the facts. Al is sort of in awe of you."

"Oh, come on." That kind of talk embarrasses me. "After three years?"

"No, I mean it. He told me once you reminded him of his big brother, who he *was* in awe of."

At that moment, I would have been hard-pressed to think of a topic I was less interested in than Al St. John's big brother. I offered to take Shirley home to Brooklyn, but she insisted on returning to the hospital. I dropped her off, then parked the Network car illegally while I made a quick pay-phone call to Lieutenant Martin's office.

Detective Gumple picked it up. Gumple had a reputation for being the best one-man tail in the history of the New York Police Department. The consensus was he did it by scent; he sure didn't do it on brain power.

I asked for Lieutenant Martin or Detective Rivetz; neither was in. "Everybody's gotta sleep sometime," Gumple told me.

"A noble sentiment," I yawned. I told him about the trashing of Harris's apartment.

"What are you telling us for? This is the homicide squad."

I could picture Gumple (who resembles a mole) pulling his ear and wrinkling his nose in consternation that I had dialed the wrong number.

I tried to put him at ease. "The lieutenant will want to know about this," I assured him. "It might be connected to the Dinkover case." That wasn't exactly a lie. If Harris's place had been left alone, I would have been *convinced* there was a connection; as it was, I just thought there might be.

"The lieutenant will want to talk to you about this," Gumple warned.

Everybody wanted to talk to me. It was heartwarming to be so popular.

"I know," I said. "And I want to talk to him, too, but not till three o'clock this afternoon. I'm going to get some sleep myself."

"I don't know, this Dinkover guy was a big shot, pretty important. I wouldn't want to tell the lieutenant—"

"Just tell him if he wants to talk to me before I get some goddam sleep, he'd better bring a warrant. And if he does, I'll just go to Riker's and sleep there." I hung up, yawned again, got in the car, and drove home.

"Home" was the Central Park West (Eighth Avenue in the poorer neighborhoods) co-op belonging to Rick and Jane Sloan. Rick and Jane had surprised me; I'd known them since college, and they'd always seemed nothing more than pleasant but basically inconsequential drones living on old family money. Then, a few years ago, they had discovered archaeology, when they decided to see how the vast amounts of money they donated to the museum were spent. They were so impressed, they took off with an expedition (which they also financed) and had been gone ever since, doing coolie labor in a leech-infested rain forest in Thailand.

In the meantime, I got custody of a fabulously expensive place to live in one of New York's ritziest neighborhoods. I enjoyed it a lot—so much that I was getting spoiled. When Rick and Jane finally came back, and I had to live some place I could afford, I was going to feel like Cinderella. I wasn't looking forward to it.

I also, for the time being, had custody of Spot, Jane's purebred Samoyed, also fabulously expensive, especially after what they'd spent on obedience training and attack training. Not that I had any complaints. Spot had saved my life more than once.

It looked as if I had just gotten home in time to save his. As usual, he started to yip as soon as I put my key in the lock. Then, as soon as I opened the door, he sprinted past me, ran to the elevator, and began to yip again.

Spot looked reproachfully at me. I felt guilty about leaving him so long without walking him, and Spot's eyes and body language reinforced the guilt. He didn't actually cross his legs and jump up and down, but he left no doubt that I hadn't gotten there a moment too soon.

Outside, Spot took care of business, then I cleaned up after him (Spot and I have never violated the great New York poop-scoop law—good citizens both of us). After that I tried to make up for my night of neglect by taking him on a nice little walk around the block. It was a brisk morning, sharp and cold and clear below an overcast sky.

Samoyeds were bred in Siberia to be sled dogs, so Spot really enjoyed himself. His perpetual smile was wider, his small pointy ears pricked up and alert, and his fluffy pure-white fur ruffled in the wind. I felt a little better about things, myself.

It was daylight now, but nobody was on the streets yet except a few deliverymen and joggers. I tried to ignore them, but Spot was more than willing to exchange cheery hellos. It got on my nerves after a while, but I let it go on until I was in danger of waking up.

Back at the apartment, I stripped and took a shower, watching as my blood and Dinkover's washed off my hands and mingled as it went down the drain. I get morbid when I'm tired.

I turned off the water, dried my hair, pulled on a pair of briefs, and collapsed on my bed. I think I was awake to feel my face hit the pillow, but it was close.

I woke up at a quarter to two, sooner than I would have liked but later than I expected. After a minimum of yawning and swearing, I rose to face what was left of the day.

I fed Spot, then punched buttons on my answering machine to see who was mad at me today. Lieutenant Martin was fairly angry; I was to be in his office tonight at seven sharp. A lot of people at the Network were angry, according to Jasmyn Santiago, my secretary, especially

Falzet and the Public Relations department. My mother was pretty upset at me for getting involved in another murder case. She thinks I do it on purpose. She also reminded me I had to come to church on Christmas day to hear my sister sing in the choir. I love my sister, but there was a longstanding rift between me and church. It was something I'd have to think about.

The only person who wasn't mad at me was Wendy Ichimi, who wanted me to call her at the Garden anytime before two fifty, which was when she was scheduled to go on for the Wednesday matinee of the ice show. She even said please.

I dialed the number she left and waited while somebody went to get her. I got the impression they weren't too crazy about phone calls in the dressing room while the show was going on, but Wendy's name carried enough weight to get things done.

While I waited, I wondered how she'd gotten my home number. It's listed, but under Rick's name. Then I remembered that I'd given the number to Max Brother last night as a gesture of the Network's full commitment to his client's welfare and similar horseshit. It seemed so long ago.

"Mr. Cobb?" Wendy's voice came. "I'm sorry it took so long to get to the phone. I was putting on my costume."

I told her it was all right. "What can I do for you."

"I really would like to talk to you today. I've got something I have to tell somebody, and after yesterday, I think you're the person. Do you mind?"

"Not at all," I lied. At this point, I minded anything that had me awake, but work was work.

"I want this to be *private*," she said.

"That can be arranged. Have you eaten?"

"Are you crazy? I have to skate! I'll be ravenous after the show, though."

"Good. Have you ever had Afghani food?"

"Not lately. You're pulling my leg, right?"

"Hey, this is New York. When is the show over, three thirty?"

"Twenty after. Meet me at the players' entrance at the Garden. Do you know where that is?"

"I've played basketball there."

"No kidding?" She sounded impressed.

"I would never kid a star. Dress casually."

"Um . . . I can't manage casual unless I go back to the hotel first. How about sloppy?"

"Sloppy is even better."

After the call to Wendy was finished, I used the phone again, this time in an attempt to mollify Mom by promising to hear my sister sing at a rehearsal or something. It did not work, but at least I tried. Then I got dressed. I tried to split the difference between sloppy and casual with a pair of jeans and bulky black turtleneck sweater. With my snorkel jacket over it, all I needed was a pipe to make me look like one of those guys who sail around the world all by themselves for no particular reason. Next, I got Spot into his silver-studded collar and leash, took him outside and walked him around awhile, then went to meet the star.

"To explore strange new worlds . . ."
—William Shatner, *Star Trek* (NBC)

CHAPTER SIX

"What a beautiful dog!" Wendy Ichimi gushed as we clambered into a taxi on Seventh Avenue. "But why do you call him Spot?"

I sighed. Somehow, I had hoped Wendy would be different. *Everybody* gushes over Spot. I know how to say "what a beautiful dog" in eleven languages. Everybody also wants to know how a pure white dog comes to be named Spot, which means I have to tell everybody. I have Rick Sloan to thank for this—it was his idea.

"He's named for the gigantic white spot that covers his entire body," I explained.

"That's silly," Wendy said. "Cute, but silly." She patted Spot, who proceeded to lick her face.

She told him to stop, giggling all the while. She was wearing jeans and an olive drab army jacket with about a million pockets. No hat, no makeup. She looked about thirteen years old and a million miles removed from the grim-faced woman who had told me she wasn't a bitch. There was a lot to Wendy Ichimi; at least more than a first impression would show. All of a sudden I was looking forward to lunch.

"You should be honored," I told her when Spot finally desisted. "He doesn't lick just any old body, you know. That shows you're all right by him."

"He's all right by me, too." She wiped her face on the sleeve of her jacket. "He's just a little damp." She stroked his head again. "I've always liked dogs, but with all the traveling I've always done, it would be silly to own one."

"How long *have* you been traveling?"

"Since just after my father married Helena."

"Since you were what? Ten?"

"Six. I was almost nineteen when I won the gold medal. When are we going to be there? I'm digesting my own stomach by now."

"We're there," I said. I had the cab driver pull over to the southwest corner of Second Avenue and St. Marks place in the East Village, paid him, and got out.

I don't get to the East Village that frequently, but then I don't have to. Things there somehow got frozen in time circa 1970. I mean, Wendy and I saw five guys who looked like Jesus in the half block we walked from the corner to our destination. If she wanted to be unnoticed, this was the place to be.

I tied Spot to a railing outside the Cafe Kabul, and we went in. Late afternoon was the quiet time of the day there, so the low table by the window, with the floor cushions and the view of the passing show, was available.

"This is neat," Wendy said, easing herself down to the cushion. She winced twice in the process.

"Are you all right?" I asked.

"Oh, sure. Arthritic knee. Inconvenient, but the doctor says I might as well skate on it as walk on it. For a little while, anyway."

"Does it give you a lot of pain?"

"Not much." She dropped her voice to a whisper. *"I keep it under control with an illegal drug."*

"This is the neighborhood for it." Out on the sidewalk, Spot watched in fascination as a black man with dreadlocks lit a joint the size of a Tootsie Roll and walked calmly on.

I turned back to Wendy, who said, "Not that kind of drug. No good for pain."

"Seriously, what are you using, DMSO?"

"That's it. How did you know?"

"Makes sense. Lots of athletes use it."

"It really helps. I don't know why they're not allowed to sell it as medicine."

"A glitch in the bureaucratic machinery. The Network news magazine show did a big report on it a while back." I explained to Wendy that DMSO—she already knew that it stood for dimethylsulfoxide—had been developed as a solvent, which was still the only legal use for it, aside for some veterinary applications. Then they discovered its pain relieving properties and sent it to the FDA for tests. That's where the trouble started. Nothing can be approved as a medicine until it passes what's called a double-blind test. That means some patients get the real stuff being tested, and others get something harmless and inert. It's called "double-blind" because neither the doctor giving the medicine, nor the patient, is allowed to know which is which.

"Unfortunately, you can't test DMSO that way," I said.

"Why not?"

"Because the DMSO, since it penetrates your skin and gets into your system so fast, has an unavoidable side effect."

"That garlic taste. I always get this fishy, garlicky taste when I use it."

"Exactly."

"Why don't they just give the patients a clove of garlic to chew on before they run the test?"

I looked at her. "That is a great idea. I wonder if they ever thought of it."

Our waitress, a tall, wide-eyed girl in loose wool pants and a brocade vest over a turtleneck, brought water and menus. As she left, the sound system started playing twangy music with unusual rhythms. Wendy made gentle movements of her head in time to them, and her sleek black hair danced for me.

"Well, you'll have a lot nicer garlic taste in your mouth in a minute," I told her. "The food here is really good."

"Why don't you order for us, then?"

"If you like."

"I like, believe me. You know, it's incredible. Practically every town I go to, the arena management or somebody wants to go to a Japanese restaurant—and I'm supposed to order for them, too. Tell you another secret—the idea of eating raw fish makes me want to barf, heritage or no heritage."

I smiled at her. "Okay. Not many fish in Afghanistan, raw or otherwise. Landlocked. I'm going to get us a sambusa appetizer then ashuk for the main dish."

"Sounds exotic."

"Sambusa is sort of like a taco shell, only it's closed all around. It's got this ground-up vegetable mixture inside. You dip it in a yogurt sauce with garlic and mint, and it's great."

"And what's the stuff that sounds like a sneeze?"

"Ashuk. That's a thin pasta stuffed with scallions, with yogurt and a meat sauce on it. The sauce is the best part. They give you pita to wipe up what's left."

"I know what pita is." She drummed fingers on the table. "This would be interesting music to skate to," she said. "Yes, Mr. Cobb, that sounds fine."

I told her to call me Matt, and she agreed on the condition I call her Wendy. That taken care of, I gave the waitress our order.

"Okay, Wendy. The next decision is up to you. Is this a show biz lunch or a people lunch?"

She tilted her head. "What's the difference?"

"In a show biz lunch, we could be making a billion-dollar deal, but we wouldn't say a word about it until dessert. A people lunch, you just tell me what's on your mind, and I react."

"Oh. Yeah, I know what you mean. Max has got to be the world champion at show biz lunches."

I nodded. "If it's not Max, it's some other agent."

"Let's make it a people lunch, then."

"Fine with me. I *was* a people, before I went to work for the Network."

"You're still a people as far as I'm concerned."

"Nice of you to say so." The waitress came with the sambusa. I took one, dipped it into the yogurt mixture. Wendy did the same, caught a drip of yogurt on her tongue before it could fall into her lap, took a bite, and smiled.

"This is good. Now I have two reasons to be grateful to you."

"Two?"

She nodded grimly. "Look, Mr. Cobb—"

"Matt."

"Oh, right. I forgot. Look, Matt. I'm afraid."

"Of what?" I asked. I wasn't sarcastic; I just wanted to know.

"I don't know. Bad publicity. The police. The way Dinkover dragged himself over to that eagle. Nightmares. Maybe I'm afraid the killing isn't over."

I froze with a sambusa at my lips. I put it down slowly and looked into Wendy's almond eyes. "Do you know something?"

"I don't know *anything!*" She frowned, and looked at me helplessly. "I used to think I'd be *happy* when Dinkover died. I hated him, you know."

"I could see you weren't too broken up about his death last night."

"Oh, I was terrible about that. I was so afraid. I get bitchy when I'm afraid."

"You must have been petrified."

She smiled. "Thanks a lot." Then, serious again, she said, "But I *was*, Matt. The idea that somebody had been around the rink. How do we know it was *Dinkover* the killer was after?"

"Got me," I said. "How do we know the waitress isn't a spy from the Ice Capades? I mean, is just a formless dread, not that I blame you if it is, or have you actually been threatened or something?"

"Oh, *threatened,*" she said, dismissing it with a graceful hand. "Everybody famous gets threatened. It got pretty bad before the Olympics, you know. A lot of people are still fighting World War II."

She gasped and put a hand to her mouth and looked so generally horrified, I thought she'd swallowed the wrong way. That was all I needed—GOLD MEDAL WINNER CHOKES ON EXOTIC FOOD WHILE TV EXEC LOOKS ON. I was about to leap the table and execute the Heimlich maneuver when Wendy spoke.

"My God," she breathed, "listen to me. That's *him* talking. I'm beginning to sound like *him.*"

"Who? Dinkover?"

She nodded.

"He killed my father, you know." She said it in the same tones a child coming home from his first Sunday school class would say, "God made the world." A basic article of faith, not to be questioned.

I questioned it anyway.

"I mean it, he tormented us. All of us. He made my father's life hell. He made my life hell. He pretended to be our friend all the while, but he was killing us."

Wendy paused while the waitress brought the ashuk. I had her refill our water glasses; Wendy took a long drink and began to speak again.

She began by telling me about her father. Henry Ichimi had been a shy and sensitive man, a second-generation American who had spent his teen years behind barbed wire in a detention camp for Japanese Americans during World War II.

"I wonder what that must have been like," Wendy said. "I don't want to know, I just wonder. I'll tell you this, though, Matt, it must have done something to him. He tried to deny his heritage. You know, I never found out until after he was dead that my father spoke fluent Japanese. He never spoke it around the house, not even to my mother.

"That was another thing. Shows how mixed up my father was. He left college to join the army to fight in Korea—you know my father was a math professor?"

I told her I'd heard it somewhere.

"Yeah, well he didn't get his degree or start to teach for a long time —he was in the army until 1955, and then what did he do but come home with a Japanese wife.

"It must have been pretty bizarre for her, don't you think? I mean, they were married for six years before I was born, and my mother still didn't speak very good English when I started to learn to speak.

"My mother had a tough pregnancy with me—she'd had two miscarriages earlier—and she never really got over giving birth. She died when I was four, and her memory comes in pretty hazy these days. Poor, uncomfortable-looking woman, trying to be a good little Japanese wife to a man who was trying hard to pretend he wasn't Japanese at all. Do you know what I remember best about her?"

I shook my head.

"I don't know how old I was. I bet I wasn't three years old yet. But I remember my mother trying to teach me a few words of Japanese; I remember the way she stood there and took it when my father reamed her out—in English—when he caught her at it."

There were tears on her face. "I wish I could remember what those damned words were. I—I'm sorry." She wiped her eyes with a corner of her napkin.

"Anyway," she went on, "my mother died. Daddy was miserable over it, but he got a promotion at the university and got involved in his work, and before long he'd met Helena. She was teaching Spanish when they met. They married two years later.

"She's a good woman, Matt, she really is. In a way, I owe her a lot—hell, I owe her everything. She's the one who started me skating. She's always been there when I needed her, even during her marriage to Speir—boy, what a creep *he* was. I just wish I could . . ."

There was a long pause which led me to wonder what Wendy just wished she could. The conclusion could be anything from the natural ". . . show her how grateful I am," to ". . . love her," to ". . . get her to buy me a salami sandwich," or something even more ridiculous. Life is full of these irritating little unsolved mysteries.

Wendy shook it off. "Anyway, it looked like my father had a good shot at being happy at last. He was the head of the math department at a great American university, respect from American colleagues included. He had an American wife. His daughter was starting to show prowess in a sport. That's a great American way for parents to get happy."

"You were about six at the time, right? You've done a lot of thinking about this since."

Wendy rolled her eyes and made a noise that was halfway between a laugh and a choke.

"Oh, yes. Quite a bit of thinking.

"Because *this* was the situation Dinkover moved in on. Not right away—about a year or so later. And he went to work on my father. And on me."

To hear Wendy tell it, Dr. Paul Dinkover had been a graduate *summa cum laude* from the Iago School for Fiendish Manipulators. He'd first approached the Ichimis in the name of Science—he wanted to test bright children like Wendy to see how well they adjusted to their intelligence, he said. Over months and years, he had preyed on Henry Ichimi's fears and frustrations. Into discussions on Jungian symbolism (something that fascinated Wendy's father) Dinkover would slip questions. Didn't it bother him that people talked behind his back about him and his white wife? Did he ever worry that he became department chairman because he would be a visible minority member in an important position and thus would make the school look good? Or did it occur to him that, with that having happened, he had probably gone as far as he would ever go? How could he trust a society who had locked its citizens up only for the crime of being of Japanese descent? And did he really think it couldn't happen again?

"Daddy became impossible to live with, Matt. The older I got, the worse he was. I could never have any friends—they were either sucking up to me because I was the best young skater in the state, or they were patronizing me because I was Japanese.

"And nobody could say a word against Dinkover, even after he moved on and started traveling for his anti-war stuff. 'He's a psychiatrist,' Daddy would say. 'He knows about these things.' He'd pay little visits, as if to give my father's paranoia a booster shot.

"Helena saw what was happening; she used to tell him what Dinkover was doing to him. He wouldn't listen, and *I* sided with him. In those days, I did. I never realized what the real problem was until after my father killed himself."

She took another drink of water.

"Do you know what hara-kiri means, Matt? It means 'belly-cutting.' At the last minute, my father decided to reassert his ethnic identity.

"Helena found the body. I don't think I could have stood it—I'd be in a nuthouse now if I'd been the one. He left a note. Nobody's seen the note outside of me and Helena and the local cops. What it mostly said was that he loved me and he was 'grateful to Paul Dinkover for his friendship and guidance.'

"When I heard that, that's when it all came to me. That's when I first realized all the things I've just been telling you. Dinkover *guided* my father, all right. He guided him to death."

I remember thinking that Wendy, in her grief, had oversimplified the matter. She'd probably transferred a lot of her own guilt onto Dinkover, too. And I don't think anybody commits suicide just because someone hits the right keys to make him depressed. Still, of all the things I'd heard about the late Dr. Dinkover, I'd never heard he was famous for his sensitivity toward the feelings of others.

Wendy read my mind. "He lived on the feelings of others, Matt. He was a vampire. He *did* know how the human mind worked; he knew how to kick out all the supports a person had built; and I swear, Matt, he liked to hear the crash."

"And I suppose your father is not the only person he did it to."

"My father is the only one I could name for certain, but I could suggest a few others."

"For instance?"

"For instance his first wife. Don't you think he set her up before he waltzed off with that younger woman? And wait till you meet *her.*"

I wondered why Wendy thought I might meet Mrs. Dinkover, but I didn't get a chance to ask her; she was still speeding along.

"And what about Velda Delinski, June Lathen, John Free, and Cyril Guzick?"

"Who are they?"

"The Landover Four."

"Oh. Yes, I can see your point. Dinkover egged them into doing something 'important' for the anti-war movement—"

"Yeah. The war stank, but believe me, Dinkover stank worse. He used things. He used the legitimate protest to feed his habit."

"—and they wind up in a federal pen on a felony murder rap when they tapped the guard at the records site a little too hard."

"John Free wound up dead," Wendy told me. "He was stabbed to death in a fight over a bar of soap last month."

"Yeah, I read about that, too. Remind me I never want to go to prison."

"Sometime prison comes to you," Wendy said. Her voice sounded very old. "That's how I felt when he cornered me in your office that afternoon."

"Yesterday afternoon," I said.

"My God. All right, yesterday. There I was, between shows, just coming up to meet my bodyguard—how is Harris, by the way?"

"I don't know. I should have called the hospital when I got up, but I didn't. He's going to live, they said last night."

"I'm glad. This is just more terribleness for you to deal with."

"I'm used to it," I said.

"But anyway, there I am, and in comes this . . . this *man*—I mean, how did he even know I was *there?*—and he just comes out and tells me I *have* to help him with his new project. *I* have to help him."

Wendy started to tremble, especially her hands. She took out a cigarette, put it in her mouth, then missed it three times with her lighter before she finally got it started.

She took a deep drag and said, "I was so stunned. I just stood there looking at him, like a bird in front of a snake or whatever it is. I was blinking my eyes hoping he'd go away. I don't even know what he was talking about. I just remember *you* made him go away. That's the other thing I have to be grateful to you about."

He had been talking to her about bilingual education, a project, in my opinion, designed to keep the downtrodden sentenced to a life in ghettos. That way, they form a captive constituency, cut off from most forms of education or enlightenment, and the people who prevent their assimilation remain in power as their only spokesmen.

Sorry. I'll get off my hobby horse. It really doesn't matter what I think of the issue. I only mention it because if Dinkover hadn't picked one of my pet peeves to harangue an obviously distraught Wendy, I probably would have been more polite, and Wendy wouldn't have been grateful to me.

Dinkover's plan was something like this. He would get somebody to hold a hearing, or a town meeting, or something like that, and Wendy would get up and say what he would tell her to say, to the effect that her life was empty, that she felt worthless as a person despite her fame, because she was cut off from her Japanese heritage and stuck only with the corrupt, plastic, evil American one. This was supposed to go over real big coming from a gold medal winner.

Judging from what Wendy had told me this afternoon, the old Master Manipulator had lost his touch with age. I mean, it's great keeping in touch with an ethnic heritage—you should hear what "Cobb" was before Ellis Island people shortened it for my great-grandfather—and maybe Wendy regretted not being more knowledgeable about her own.

But it would be hard to think of an appeal from that old man to that young woman less likely to work than that one.

I sat there listening to it, and the whole thing was incredible. There was Dinkover, tall, old, dignified in a fanatical kind of way, shaking a liver-spotted finger in Wendy's face as she stood at my side.

"Look at you," he said. "You're one of the most famous Japanese Americans alive, yet look at you. You don't know how to read Japanese. You don't know how to write Japanese. You don't know how to *speak* Japanese!"

Being very helpful, I put my hand on his arm and said sincerely, "But, boy, she really knows how to *look* Japanese, doesn't she?"

It brought down the house. Harris laughed. Jazz laughed. Shirley, who'd been moping because of Harris's flirtation with Wendy, laughed. Wendy went into hysterics. Even Al St. John risked a chuckle.

Dinkover didn't like being laughed at. He'd turned an angry red and tightened his lips as if to shout but thought better of it. He'd straightened his tie, spun on his heel, and stormed from the office, walking very quickly and heavily for an old man.

And that was the last I had seen of him until I found his body on the ice.

We were quiet for a while, mopping up the last of the yogurt and tomato sauce with pita. The waitress came and took our plates away. I asked Wendy if she wanted any dessert or coffee.

"No thanks, I've probably eaten too much already. I have to skate again tonight."

I started making arrangements for the Network to pick up the lunch tab. Wendy patted her lips with a napkin and said, "God, I wish I'd known you could chase Dinkover away by laughing at him. That was the first time I'd ever seen him chased away before he was ready to go. He was so . . . so *relentless*. Once he thought of something, he usually never gave up."

I nodded. "Right up until the end," I said. "It took somebody pretty relentless to make it across that ice."

"When he went for the eagle, you mean."

We were outside now. Wendy would have walked right on, but I asked her to wait while I untied Spot.

"Oh, poor puppy. I forgot all about him."

"He didn't mind. I took peeks through the window. He had all the girls in the East Village making a fuss over him while we were inside."

I reached into my pocket for my gloves, then cursed when I remembered I didn't have any.

"What's the matter?" Wendy asked.

"Nothing. But why do you say he went for the eagle? You said it twice."

"Well, he had it in his hand, didn't he? I didn't see the body—thank God—but that's what all the newspapers said. Wasn't it?"

"I only got a bleary-eyed look at them before I went to bed," I told her, "but it seemed to me the emphasis was on the flag. The irony of it and all that."

"I'm sure they mentioned the eagle."

Spot was loose now. I asked Wendy if she wanted to take a little walk. She said sure, and we turned east, back toward Second Avenue.

"I'm sure they did. What I'm wondering about is why you latched onto it."

"I don't know. It's just what stuck in my mind."

"I only ask because it's sort of perched in my mind, too, and I'm damned if I know why."

Then we talked about other things, everyday things like how she liked New York (a lot), and how she wanted to retire from skating, or at least from traveling, in another year or so. She asked me about myself, and pretended to be impressed when she heard that I'd been an NCAA division II second-team basketball All-American, and things like that.

It was nice, walking along through the cold with the pretty, bright, unique individual at my side. I was just reflecting how pleasant it all was.

When hell broke loose.

"So don't be surprised if someday, somewhere, some time when you least expect it . . ."

—Allen Funt, *Candid Camera* (CBS)

CHAPTER SEVEN

My first thought was that it was a Mafia hit. A big black car squealed up to the curb next to us. Wendy jumped into me, startled. Spot ran toward the car, snarling, waiting for me to give him the kill command.

The door to the car jumped open, as if pushed by the loud voice that came from within.

"There she is! There is my pupil! And the tall hoodlum with the dog has kidnapped her! I demand you summon the police! No! There is no time! We will seize them and yell for the police!"

It went on that way, a series of explosions like a car with no muffler. They got louder as the owner of the voice got out of the car. He was dressed magnificently in a sable jacket and one of those Russian hats, which was appropriate, because this was Ivan Danov.

"Oh, Mr. Danov," Wendy said. If it's possible to gasp and laugh, that's what Wendy was doing.

"Do not fear; this is America. You will be rescued! Police! Police!"

I was somewhat taken aback by the dramatic entry, but I was beginning to put things together. This wasn't a Mafia car; it belonged to that other sinister, all-pervasive influence in American life: The Network.

"Relax, Mr. Danov. Consider yourself to have made a citizen's arrest. Let's get in the car, Wendy."

"You!" Danov said. He had fought his way out of the car at last, but we spun him around and put him right back in again, this time in the back seat. Wendy gave me a conspiratorial look and climbed in there

with him. That left me the front seat and the companionship of Al St. John.

Al's boyish face said he was disappointed in me, but his voice was apologetic. "I'm sorry I had to hunt you down like this, Matt, but the Mad Russian there was all set to call the cops."

I was finding out for the first time that the Mad Russian could talk in something less than a shout—right now he was chewing out Wendy in a hissing whisper that sounded like a clothesline whipping in a gale. Every once in a while, I would catch a phrase, like *"you know you must report to me after every performance"* or ". . . leave me to think you are lying dead in a filthy street!"

Wendy took it all indulgently; apparently this wasn't the first time she and her coach had played out a scene like this. She caught me looking at her in the rearview mirror and winked.

I tuned out and gave my full attention to Al. "You did the right thing," I told him. "I just want to know how you found me."

"I talked to Bea Dunney—Wendy's friend in the show—"

"I know who she is."

"Oh, right, I'd forgotten. Anyway, I spoke to her, and she said she thought you were taking Miss Ichimi out to lunch, that she wanted to talk to you. It was a long shot, but I remembered where you'd taken *me* for lunch when I first came to work for the Network; I figured it was a favorite place of yours and that you might be there. What I really wanted to do was to get Mr. Danov—" he lowered his voice, "to get Mr. Danov in a car and away from telephones. He was really getting crazy, Matt."

"I'll have to hang around with you more, Al."

"Why's that?" It was hard to tell if he liked the idea or not.

"Your hunches pay off."

"But . . . um . . . Matt . . . I, well, Good Lord, I wouldn't have needed to *get* a hunch if you'd remember to keep your beeper with you!"

His face was flushed with real anger, and I wanted to laugh at him, but I didn't, for two reasons. One, I'd been trying to loosen him up since he'd come to work for me, and this was the first sign of success there'd been, and two, he was right. I promised him I'd try harder in the future—no, by God, that I would absolutely carry my beeper about at all times, so there.

I asked him how Harris was.

"No change. Shirley called from the hospital, but I think more because she needed company than because she had any news."

"She doesn't take it easy, *she's* going to wind up in the hospital."

We dropped Wendy and Danov at the hotel. Danov thanked us with a grunt—about halfway there, he'd stopped abusing Wendy and gone into a sulk. Wendy walked around to my window and knocked on it. When I rolled it down she said, "Come see the show tonight."

I thought it over for a second. "I will if I can. I don't know how long the cops are going to keep me."

"Oh. Well, I'm only on in the last half hour. Come if you can make it. I'll leave word at the box office. You come, too, Al."

Al smiled at her. "I'm working tonight. I'll take in a matinee sometime."

"Sure, I can arrange that," she said. "See you tonight, Matt, maybe. I'll keep my fingers crossed."

My brain told me it was time to pay a call on Lieutenant Martin, and my watch confirmed it. I gave myself a silent cheer, then told Al to turn the car around and head back south.

"I want to introduce you to my police friends," I said.

"*Why?*" he demanded. His voice cracked with it. He didn't even say good Lord.

"You've worked here long enough for it to happen," I told him. "It's really kind of a fluke you haven't had to deal with the police before now. Besides, with Harris laid up and Shirley . . . preoccupied, you are *it* as far as the department goes. I can't pull Kolaski or Smith off the Poland thing can I? Of course not."

"Well, sure, Matt, I'm honored in a way. Just a little surprised."

"Where's your ambition? I'm not going to live forever, you know."

He looked at me strangely. "What kind of talk is that, for crying out loud?"

"Silly," I conceded. "But I may retire, and not at age sixty-five, either. I can get weary of this job sometimes. Besides, maybe I just want to keep you around in case you have another hunch. What could an eagle mean?"

Al looked out the windshield and kept driving.

"Yo," I said. "Hello there. Earth, calling Al St. John. Come in, Al."

He showed me a sheepish smile. "I thought you were just thinking out loud. You do that a lot, you know."

"As a matter of fact, I didn't. Hazard of living alone, I guess. But no, I wasn't thinking out loud. I was wondering if you had any hunches about eagles."

"I thought he was . . . I thought Dinkover went after the flag. Sort of a final gesture of contempt. Isn't that what the cops think?"

"Don't spread this around, but the cops have been known to be wrong. *Now* I'm thinking out loud. I don't know if the cops are wrong or not. Wendy Ichimi seems to have convinced herself it's the eagle that's important; I'm trying to figure out if there's anything to it."

Al shrugged, but he was willing to play. "It could be a name, or part of a name. Egelton, Egelman, something like that. Maybe."

"Maybe. It's something to check out." I scratched my head. "The trouble is, eagles are symbolic of so many things. Banks. Condensed milk."

"Lots of countries, too. Including this one. Maybe it was the eagle, Matt, but it could still be a gesture of contempt. With his dying breath, he pulls down the flag *and* the eagle. Two symbols for the price of one, you know what I mean?"

"It's a point, but let's not close the deal completely, yet." Al was silent. I looked at him, saw him making a face with tight lips. I remember resenting it, telling him that this job involved imagination as much as anything else, and he might as well keep in practice.

"It just seems like such a waste of time."

"A great advertising man once said fifty percent of everything he did was wasted—unfortunately, it was impossible to tell which fifty percent.

"Come on, now. The United States is symbolized by an eagle. Poland. Who else?"

"Nazi Germany. There's a possibility. God knows a Nazi, or anybody right-wing, would have reason to kill Dinkover."

"Yeah," I said, "only trouble is, to Dinkover, everybody to the right of Ho Chi Minh was a Nazi." I sighed. "I think ancient Rome used an eagle, too."

Al grunted.

"Well," I said, "that simplifies matters. We're looking for a Polish American Nazi from ancient Rome. I guess we can put this little exercise in the wasted fifty percent, huh?"

Al grinned. "Here's headquarters," he said.

"Okay, but I'll keep thinking about it. Maybe Wendy will remember why she thought of it."

Lieutenant Martin was sitting at his desk, hunched over a messy Reuben sandwich, trying to keep corned beef juice, sauerkraut, melted Swiss cheese, and Russian dressing from dripping on his pants.

"Why don't you put the wrapping paper on your lap," I suggested, "instead of giving yourself a hunchback?"

He took another bite and looked up past his eyebrows at me. It was a dirty look, but he moved the shiny white paper to his lap and sat up.

"How's the sandwich?" I asked.

"It's delicious. And I have the added pleasure of watching my arteries harden before my very eyes. I ought to have you arrested."

"Well," I said. "I wasn't expecting a fatted calf or anything, but this is a little extreme."

"The charge is being too goddam contrary to be allowed to run around loose. When I want to talk to you, you're nowhere around. Now that I finally get two seconds to take a break and have something to eat, you show up early."

"I could leave again."

"Right. Then I'd get a postcard from Sydney, Australia, telling me you'll talk to me when you get back. No, Matty, why don't you just hang around for a while? Now that I know where you are. Rivetz will be back with the lab reports in a minute, maybe there'll be something there to help." That was supposed to be funny. Something about police work makes men sardonic.

He took another bite and chewed. After a few seconds, he gestured at Al with a finger shiny with drippings. "Does your friend here talk, or am I supposed to think he's just a hallucination?"

"Oh. I'm sorry, I'm forgetting my manners."

Just then, Rivetz walked in, giving forth with a snort as he did so. Whether at the idea of my manners, or the idea of manners in general, I've never been able to decide.

"I ignore extraneous noises," I said. "Lieutenant, Rivetz, this is Al St. John, of my Special Projects gang. I wanted him to see the police in their native habitat."

"Ha," the lieutenant said. Rivetz snorted again. They told Al they were glad to meet him. The lieutenant said he hoped they'd see more of him, especially if it meant seeing less of me.

"Has he driven you crazy yet?" Mr. M. asked. "He's been doing it to me for twenty-four years now."

I was glad to see all this. Lieutenant Martin only goes out of his way to insult me when he's in a particularly good mood.

"He usually has a dog with him," the lieutenant said.

"We left him downstairs. Any results on the case?"

He asked me why I wanted to know.

"You seem so full of whatever it is you tend to get full of."

"Thank you, I think. No, I'm full of what I'm full of because I just fixed up two of the most obnoxious women on the planet with each other, getting them out of *my* nappy hair for at least one glorious night."

"Who is this?"

"Mrs. Paul Dinkover. Matty, that woman should be the hemorrhoid poster child. She's been giving the department a pain in the ass since early this morning."

"Has she been here?"

"Three times. In between, she's been talking to the media. Don't you watch your own Network, for God's sake?"

"I've been busy. Who'd you foist her off on?"

"The Frying Nun."

I smiled at the thought. It was a tribute to Livia Goosens, who had abandoned the convent for law school, and who was now an assistant district attorney, that she had acquired her nickname despite the lack of a capital punishment law in New York. She brought to the law all the knuckle-smashing implacability she'd used in teaching Catholic school. It hadn't made her loved in either place. It had, however, given her an eighty-nine percent conviction record and a rep big enough, it seemed, to have her put in charge of the Dinkover prosecution, when and if Lieutenant Martin gave her somebody to prosecute.

It made for an interesting picture, and I told the lieutenant so. "Only one thing. What if they team up?"

A look of genuine fear came to his face, then passed. "No, they're both too ornery. Jesus, Matty, don't say things like that while I'm eating."

Rivetz's instinct told him the byplay had run its course. He cleared his throat and said, "I got the lab results here. Took a look at them on the way over."

"I figured you would. Anything?"

"Nothing on Dinkover, except the killer is one cold son of a bitch. The way the medical examiner figures it, our little playmate stuck the knife in—big hunting knife, blade two inches across. Untraceable, of course."

"I thought it was a big one when I saw the handle," I said.

"Well, you were right," Rivetz said irritably. He hates to be interrupted. "The killer stuck in the knife right below the belly button, then held it there while Dinkover sliced himself down on it with his own weight. Right up to the sternum."

"Cold and *strong*," Martin said. "Dinkover was old, but he was no flyweight. Sounds like we're looking for a man."

"A woman could do it, if she wanted to badly enough," I said.

"She could hold the knife in both hands," Al St. John offered. It was the first thing he'd said since pleased to meet you.

The lieutenant sighed. "Yeah, actually, I thought of that myself. Thirty-six years on the force, and I'm still hoping someday I'll find something easy. Rivetz, tomorrow, call the lab and ask them about this."

"Right," Rivetz said. He took out a little pad and made a note. "The rest of it is routine, except, of course, for that crawl across the ice. Berkowitz at the lab says there's no doubt Dinkover did his own crawling. He also says it's the goddamnedest thing he's ever seen."

This seemed as good a time as any to bring up the eagle business. I summed up my talk with Wendy and explained about my hunch. "After all," I concluded, "she'd known him practically all her life—he even did some sort of half-assed analysis of her when she was a little girl. I figure if she thinks the eagle, and not the flag, is the important part, there might be something to it."

They thought I was nuts, but they were willing to play. This proved two things: that even a cop likes a change of pace from the normal routine of investigation; and that the normal routine (stoolies, legwork, lab work, and the rest) had so far availed them, as the saying goes, nought.

They came up with a lot of the stuff Al and I had already discussed, then the lieutenant said, "The Philadelphia Eagles. Maybe he was trying to tell us the killer was a football player."

"A hockey player would be more appropriate to the setting. Too bad there's no hockey team called the Eagles," I said.

Rivetz was sarcastic. "Yeah, too bad. That would narrow it down to maybe a million people, most of them Canadians. Cobb, are we supposed to buy it that Dinkover crawled across the ice to leave us a clue to his killer's identity? That it wasn't just for some fanatic political bullshit?"

"I haven't come out and said so, but that's the general idea. It happens all the time in mystery stories. Have you read Ellery Queen?"

"It don't happen much in real life, but suppose this is it—Dinkover was weird enough for me to believe he'd do it—suppose he was telling us the killer was somebody named *Flagg;* that it didn't have anything to do with an eagle at all?"

"I think you should check it out."

Rivetz looked sheepish. "Well, actually we are." He cleared his throat. "But about this eagle stuff. You were in the army weren't you?"

I looked at Rivetz with new respect. He had more imagination than I had ever given him credit for. "Right. The army. A bird colonel. A lieutenant colonel wears a silver oak leaf; a full colonel wears an eagle. A navy captain, too."

"Yeah," the lieutenant put in, "and when it's payday, that's when the eagle shits. Hell, a lot of government employees still use that term."

Al St. John was trying not to laugh. I heard little noises escape from him, and I finally asked him what was so funny.

"I'm sorry, Matt," he said. "I just keep adding it up. Good Lord, now we're looking for a Polish American Nazi from ancient Rome, who was a paymaster in the army with the rank of colonel, or in the navy with the rank of captain, who plays professional football."

I looked around the room. Everybody was grinning. I joined in; I guessed it was pretty funny, at that.

CHAPTER EIGHT

I mulled over what Rivetz had told me about the break-in at Harris's apartment, while the desk sergeant played with Spot. The burglar there had been the weirdest combination of pro and madman any of us had ever heard of. He knew just what to steal and, as far as we could tell, had gotten away cleanly. Why, then, had he hit the place like a MIRV warhead?

The desk sergeant didn't want Spot to leave—the Samoyed hadn't exhausted his bag of tricks yet. I made a deal with him. Spot would do one more trick, his most spectacular, then the sergeant would let us go.

"Okay, boy, here we go." I put out both my hands, palms up. Spot's grin got wider. He knew what I had in mind, and he's an incurable showoff. He pranced over to me as I backed up into the middle of the room. This trick takes plenty of space.

Spot put one forepaw, then the other, on my hands. His brown eyes were shiny, and he was panting with excitement. "Ready?" I said. "One, two three, *hup!*" With hup, I lifted my arms at the same instant Spot gave a spring with his hind legs. The Samoyed went whirling backward, then spiked all four paws in a perfect landing after one of his best backflips ever.

The sergeant applauded and said Spot was smarter than half the cops they had around there.

A voice behind me said, "Very amusing." I could feel the smile slide from my face, like an egg from a greased pan. I turned and faced Livia Goosens, the Frying Nun.

"How fortunate to find you here, Mr. Cobb." She had a nice voice, deep and well modulated. In appearance, she was formidable. She was tall and heavy-boned, and her face was always red, as if yesterday had been her first day at the beach. She had gray hair that she wore in a kind of corrugated ponytail.

I had once heard a policewoman say ADA Goosens had a "strong face," that "she wouldn't look so bad if she would only Do Something with herself."

That may well be true, I'm no expert. One thing I did know—Livia Goosens was never going to Do Anything with herself. She had too much fun (or whatever it was she had) Doing Things with other people.

Right now, she was Doing Something with me.

"Is this your attempt to raise morale among city employees, Mr. Cobb? By performing animal acts for policemen?"

"Yeah," I said, "how do you like it? Tomorrow, I bring my sea lions."

She forebore to comment. "Please remain here a few moments; there's someone I want you to meet."

"I'm sorry, Ms. Goosens, but I really have to run along—"

"Mr. Cobb." She said it in such a way that the air seemed to be filled with unspoken syllables, all of them accusatory. I felt obliged to stay and face the music. I turned to Al, introduced him, and told him to beat it to the Network, or he'd be late for his shift. Then I asked Ms. Goosens what she wanted.

She smiled at me. It was a smile that had spelled doom for hundreds of lawbreakers. I was happy to realize I hadn't broken any laws lately. At least no big ones.

"It's not what *I* want," the Frying Nun modulated. She was practically purring. "You have been asked for. Specifically. And since you seem to be some sort of adjunct to the police department—"

"I wouldn't go so far as to say *that*, Ms. Goosens."

"How modest of you. Rest assured, Mr. Cobb, that all my attempts to get you out from underfoot of the law-enforcement operations of the City of New York are met with just that attitude, if not those precise words."

She did this thing with her teeth and lips that was either scorn with a large portion of smug, or smug with a goodly percentage of scorn. Smug won out when I failed to come up with a response.

"Seriously, Cobb." Now that she'd put me in my place, I no longer had to be called "mister." "Seriously, do you think that you have no special privileges around here? That any citizen off the street may *stroll* into any police building and chat about a pending investigation with the officers in charge?"

By God, I know a rhetorical question when I hear one. I kept my mouth shut.

"I assure you, that is not the case. If you tried to do these sorts of things with the district attorney's office, you would face a rude awakening, Cobb. A rude awakening."

"Well, Goosens," I said. As long as we were dispensing with the honorifics, what the hell. "Thanks for the warning. I promise never to try to do these sorts of things with the district attorney's office. Cross my heart."

"You are amazing, Cobb. Do you ever succeed in amusing anyone with your foolishness?"

I was getting really tired of this woman. "My antics have been known to raise a chortle or two. What's the point? My dog is getting hungry."

I wished Lieutenant Martin was there to see her reaction. For the first time, the Frying Nun had been Taken Aback. She was used to people staying intimidated. Little did she know that she was dealing with a man who had been thrown out of Catholic School in the fourth grade for asserting himself against a bossy nun.

I'll say this for her, she recovered quickly. She just licked her lips and went on. "My *point* is this: Since you usurp some of the privileges of a law-enforcement professional, you must be ready to assume some of the *duties* of a law-enforcement professional."

"Oh," I said. "Is that all? What's the matter, you have a car you want towed or something?"

"Or something. There is a concerned citizen you must listen to. Her complaint concerns you especially. *Mrs. Dinkover!*"

The sharp tones of her hail were like little acupuncture needles numbing my ego. I'd been set up.

Carla Nelson Dinkover (I presumed) stepped out from behind a pillar. God knows how Ms. Goosens got her to stay there. While she was still walking over to us, the DA's lady called out, "This is Cobb, Mrs. Dinkover. I hope he can satisfy you. I'm leaving now, late for mumble mumble," and she was gone.

I had to admit to a certain admiration for her. Like Lieutenant Martin, she had foisted off one problem on another, in this case, Carla Dinkover on me. The Frying Nun wins again.

I didn't brood on it. Instead, I watched the widow walk toward me. I did not stare but only because I told myself I mustn't. I knew for a fact that Carla Dinkover was about the same age Livia Goosens, i.e., pushing fifty. The difference was, Mrs. Dinkover Did Something with herself.

Lots of things. Like, she exercised a lot. That was a mature figure, but what a mature figure. She kept her hair blond—nature or chemistry made it the color of a good yellow cake, the kind with extra egg yolk. It was shoulder length and bouncy, parted on the side. Her face was made up to feature her intelligent brown eyes. She wore a bright red dress that, unlike some brightly colored clothes, called attention to her figure instead of to itself.

There was nothing about her that made a person think, wow, she looks young, or boy, for a lady pushing fifty, she's well preserved, or anything like that. She just looked *right;* she seemed to be saying, "This is exactly what I am." What she was was damned attractive.

She put out a hand. As I took it, she said, "I doubt you can, Mr. Cobb."

"Doubt I can what, Mrs. Dinkover?"

"Satisfy me."

She was smiling. Maybe she was just being nice, but I had the impression that smile was daring me to make something of it.

I took her up on it. "If you didn't think so, why did you want to see me?"

"There's always a chance. Come, Mr. Cobb, there must be more convenient places to talk than Police Headquarters."

"I've frequently thought so," I said. "Would you like to get a cup of coffee? There's a place near here."

"A drink would be better. It's been a long day. You wouldn't be ashamed to be seen in a saloon with me, would you, Mr. Cobb?"

"No. But then, I'm not in mourning."

She looked surprised for a moment, then smiled—a real smile, no dare in it this time.

"Oh, you mean this?" She indicated her dress with a graceful sweep of her hand. "Don't get the wrong idea; my husband was a great man, and I loved him very deeply. I mean to see his killer gets what he deserves. The world has been deprived of one of its finest minds."

That reads like something she felt she ought to say, but there was nothing in her voice or attitude to make me feel she was anything but sincere.

"But my husband's mind—his whole life, really—was devoted to freeing people from the tyranny of *symbols*. He tried to get the human race to see beyond flags, beyond skin colors. To get to the *reality* of things. That was where he broke with Jung. If I were to run around today in black from head to toe, it wouldn't change the reality a bit. Yesterday Paul was alive. Today he's dead. The black is only a mindless symbol of the event."

"So you counter-symbolize things by wearing the brightest color you could lay your hands on."

She stared at me as if I had a bad word written in the middle of my forehead. At last, she said, *"Touché.* You see how insidious this whole business can be. I listened to the man who wrote the gospel on getting to the truth behind the symbol for over twenty years, helping him write it, in fact, and here I am, falling into the same mindless behavior he loathed."

I told her to excuse herself; she'd been upset.

She laughed. "I think I'll take you up on that. At least, symbolic or not, it's given me something to think about."

I took her to a bar nearby, a place called the Wet Whistle. Being in the shadow of headquarters, it was inevitably a cop hangout. It was decorated with pictures of famous detectives, real and fictional. We took a table under the stern eyes of Inspector Thomas Byrnes, a cruel and efficient cop who was also an efficient and unabashed grafter. Mrs. Dinkover asked who he was; I told her, adding it had taken Theodore Roosevelt to drive him out of office.

"Things don't change, do they?" she said.

"What do you mean?"

"Cruel. Corrupt."

"Not so loud," I told her. "There are more cops within earshot here than there ever were at headquarters. Besides, some of my best friends happen to be policemen."

"So Miss Goosens told me."

The waiter came to take our order. Mrs. Dinkover ordered Wild Turkey 101 proof straight up, water back. I ordered the same on the rocks.

She smiled at me again. "Bourbon drinkers are so rare these days."

"A good American drink," I said.

"Patriotic symbolism, Mr. Cobb?"

I took a sip of iced bourbon. It cooled the front of my mouth and warmed the back. "That's right," I said. "Also, I like it."

She lifted her glass. "Also you like it," she said. "As my husband might have told you, that's the important part. To the reality behind the symbol." She sipped her drink; I took another pull at mine.

I was all set to call Lieutenant Martin a liar the next time I saw him. This woman had been so far from obnoxious I started to wonder whether we had been introduced to the same Mrs. Dinkover.

Then she showed me. "Mr. Cobb," she said sweetly, "who invited my husband to the skating rink last night? Who let him in?"

"I wish I knew," I said.

"That's not an answer."

I took another sip of bourbon. "You're right, it isn't. I was an English major in college, and you're right. *Here* is an answer. I don't know."

Now I found out what was so obnoxious about Carla Nelson Dinkover. She had these little membranes in her ear canals that filtered out anything she didn't want to hear. She was always charming, she was always calm, but she never conceded I didn't know who'd let the old man in.

She kept saying things like, "Surely you can't think I'm that naive, can you, Mr. Cobb?" and similar cajoleries. It was a skill that had probably stood her in good stead in her journalism days, but it's wasted if the cajolee is truly ignorant of what she's trying to find out.

I called her attention to this, but no good. The filters.

Then she switched tactics. She told me things about the people who were there last night. "Helena Andersen—"

"Mrs. Speir?"

"Yes, but Paul always referred to her by her maiden name and I fell into the habit as well. She and Paul had an affair, you know. Before he met me, of course." She said it with perfect confidence that after a man had tied up with her, the thought of having an affair would never cross his mind. I could see her point.

"He introduced Helena to Henry Ichimi, in fact, but I suspect Helena never really got over Paul."

"So she killed him? At that time, in that place?"

"Don't let's get ahead of ourselves. We're discussing who let him in."

"Oh, I forgot."

"Somehow, Mr. Cobb, I doubt you forget much. Then there's the agent, Max Brother."

"I didn't know he even knew your husband."

"He didn't. They only met for the first time yesterday afternoon in your office."

"Then why would he get your husband out to the rink?"

"It's a fact that Wendy Ichimi is unhappy with Max Brother as an agent."

"It's a rumor," I said. I'd heard it, but the contracts he'd negotiated about Wendy's show for the Network were ironclad, and that was all Special Projects had to know about it.

"There was an argument, though between Helena Ander—Speir and Brother about his handling of Wendy's career."

"How do you come to know this?"

"Mutual friends from California. Paul and I have kept in touch with old faculty. A friend of Paul's and mine was out to lunch with Helena when Max Brother entered the restaurant. Helena apparently couldn't hold herself back. There was quite a scene."

"What does this have to do with your husband, though?"

"Perhaps Brother wanted Paul to use his influence on Wendy to keep her from firing him."

"Perhaps," I conceded, being generous. "But there are two things wrong with it. One, Brother is an ace negotiator. He's probably got a contract with Wendy *God* couldn't find a loophole in. Two, and I mean no offense here, even if Brother *were* in danger, I doubt he'd ask your husband to use his influence. I don't mean to be offensive, here, but your husband had the same influence on Wendy Ichimi a camphor flake has on a moth. One whiff and get me out of here."

"I *know* she reacts negatively to Paul. Did react, I mean. It's only been a day, sometimes I forget Paul is . . ."

"But Wendy only acted that way because she knows my husband was right. If there weren't any truth in what Paul said, Wendy wouldn't be afraid to hear it."

"Why don't we just let her make her own accommodations with her own life, Mrs. Dinkover?"

"She's running from the *truth!*"

"She's running from your husband's truth. And whose business is it but Wendy's, anyway?"

"So that's how you see it," she said. I nodded. "What are you running from Mr. Cobb?"

I looked at my watch for effect. "You, unfortunately, Mrs. Dinkover. I have an appointment uptown."

"I'm going uptown, too. Perhaps you could drop me off."

Sure, I thought, thereby giving her more time to bend my ear in the cab. I suppressed a sigh and said I'd be delighted.

"Where are you going?" I asked.

"Madison Square Garden. I'm going to see the ice show. Wendy may be pigheaded and spoiled, but she skates like an angel."

"*Good evening, everybody, and welcome to the World's Most Famous Arena.*"

—John Condon, *Madison Square Garden Presents* (MSG Cablevision)

CHAPTER NINE

I leaned over a railing in the orange section of Madison Square Garden, looking, as it turned out, in a straight line over the head of Carla Dinkover about thirty rows away, watching Bea Dunney skate. The blond skater had looked tired and washed out the night before, but now she was glowing.

Since she wasn't a star, she didn't get just to go out and skate. She was in a comedy bit, a take off on old-time melodramas. Bea shared the spotlight with two male skaters, a mustachioed villain in a hammertail coat, and a heroic lumberjack type. The lumberjack was the weakest of the three, not through any fault of his own. Male skaters tend not to run to bulk, and lumberjacks do, so there was a credibility problem.

Still, the crowd loved it. The arena, a big hatbox of a building, was about two-thirds full, not bad for the middle of Christmas week. The crowd was mostly kids, it seemed, but there was a higher percentage of adults than I would have expected.

There was a bit of slapstick now as the villain tried to tie Bea up and put her across the railroad tracks. Splits and slides and some really amazing combinations of positions. More than that, it was well timed and funny. It was easy to see that Wendy's friend was a skillful skater with more than a little talent for physical comedy.

The melodrama skit ended, to be replaced with one of those high-kicking precision-type numbers, which I could live without. I took a walk.

I walked out to a concourse, then took an escalator up to the mezzanine level. It turned out that Wendy had arranged for more than a ticket for me; she'd gotten me something that was practically a carte blanche. I decided to use it to check in on some Network business.

The Network was going to great trouble and no little expense to do a little temporary remodeling at the Garden. Any one floor of an arena like this one tends to be built on the circle-within-a-circle plan. The outside circle is just a wall; within the other one is the arena itself. Nestled in the inside wall are concession stands, rest rooms, medical aid stations, and offices.

The Network was installing broadcast equipment in one of the offices, which was going to be used in taping Wendy's performance on Christmas Eve. There was plenty of TV equipment in the building already, of course—Madison Square Garden runs its own nationwide cable TV Network—but this was experimental stuff. Some genius (or a group of them) at Network Labs had designed a new system that would draw less power and, more important, use less light, while showing equally sharp pictures. If nothing else, it would save the Network money if this sort of thing could be adapted to our own studios. If you think *your* light bill is outrageous, get a load of the Network's someday. It's always taken an incredible amount of light to get a TV show on the air—that "hot lights" business is true—and color takes three times as much light as black and white does. All that would change if the system worked the way Network Labs promised it would.

I couldn't see any reason it shouldn't. Ickx of Belgium had done the new asymmetrical lenses, and Torahido of Japan had done all the solid state stuff. What was in it for the Garden was an early crack at the new system at a big discount, when and if it went into production.

I walked around to the room, used my big-shot key (I had keys to all Network facilities at the Garden) to open the door, and took a look around. It looked exactly like an office that had been converted to a makeshift control room, with consoles on tables, and a few desks and potted palms moved casually around the room.

I turned off the light, locked the door again, and went back into the arena just as they announced Wendy.

The crowd, who had been good-naturedly noisy during the whole performance, suddenly shut up. This was what they had been waiting for. Me too.

The arena went dark. Then, a blue spotlight shone at one end of the ice. The gate opened, and Wendy Ichimi appeared. Her face was solemn, as if to tell the world that what was coming up was important. She wore an outfit of white silk, embroidered, or embossed, or whatever the hell you call it, with flowers, also in white silk. The blue light made it all seem somehow whiter than white. At the same time the light darkened Wendy's skin. The contrast was striking.

She skated rapidly to the center of the rink, then stopped on a dime and made a deep curtsey, arms, legs, everything as graceful as a ballerina's. The applause was tremendous, then the crowd fell back into silence.

Wendy began her routine. I hadn't agreed with much Carla Nelson Dinkover had said to me that evening, but she was right about one thing—Wendy *did* skate like an angel. It would be natural, maybe even inevitable, for a skater's performance to slip once the days of competition were over, when it was show biz instead of sport, and she has to go out and do it twice a day.

There wasn't a trace of that in Wendy. She soared and spun and glided with the same grace, determination, and delicate power I'd seen her display as I sat in front of my television set watching her win the gold medal.

I started watching her with a TV man's eye—I want a camera at ice level when she dips into her Hamill Camel, to catch the way her hair falls across her face; we'd better have a long shot for that combination, to show what a distance this little person covers in one bound, that sort of thing. After about twenty seconds, I forgot all about it and let my eyes and mind fly with her.

The music was great, too, Neil Diamond's "Walk on Water," pretty, dramatic, and appropriate. I wondered who had chosen it.

The crowd stayed silent through the routine, not even clapping along with the fast parts of the music, as skating crowds are known to do. The spotlight changed color, from blue, to green, to red, and finally to a dazzling white. It followed her so closely that it looked as if she was giving off the light, glowing with her own incandescence in the darkened arena.

Finally, she did some double toe loops, then went into a spin that looked as if it were going to last forever. She almost teased the audience with it, using her arms to control her speed, spinning fast, then more slowly, then so slowly that you were sure she was going to stop; then suddenly pulling her arms in and spinning so fast she was just a dazzle of black hair and white costume and bronze legs and flashing silvery blades.

Finally she stopped. And the crowd went crazy. Including me. I had to tell myself to start breathing again.

With the applause, Wendy smiled for the first time, and that was dazzling, too.

It was easy to tell she loved it, that she was getting off on the idea that she, for a few minutes at least, owned the minds and emotions of thousands of strangers.

Wendy quartered the arena and curtseyed deeply four times. She skated off to more applause. The announcer now said it was time for the grand finale, featuring the entire company, but I didn't stay to see it. It would be another chance to see Wendy skate, briefly at least, but I wanted to get around to the athletes entrance. With the pass Wendy had left me had been a note asking me to meet her after the show. A quick look at the crowd showed me that Carla Dinkover was leaving early, too. I doubted she had an appointment with Wendy, but she might have had an idea of her own. That made me doubly eager to be at my station, in case there was a scene brewing.

It was a madhouse outside, as it always is after an event at the Garden. Seventh Avenue is a wide street, but you could walk across it on the yellow roofs of taxicabs immobilized in traffic.

It was much colder than it had been that afternoon, and there was more moisture in the air. I allowed myself to hope we might have snow for Christmas. I'm not that crazy about snow in February, which is the only month in which New York has seen snow for years, but I love it in late December. Mr. Nostalgia. It seems like there was always a white Christmas when I was a kid, but the year before, Christmas day had been sixty-three degrees and foggy. That was like no Christmas at all.

I got some suspicious looks from some of the skaters as they began to leave the building; after all, this made twice in one day they'd seen me hanging around. I was beginning to feel like a stage-door Johnny.

There was no sign of Carla Dinkover, for which I was thankful. I figured if she hadn't shown up by now, she never would, so I left my vantage point for a place near the wall that was less obvious and also out of the wind.

I spent some time trying to understand the doctor's widow. On the one hand, twenty years my senior or not, she was a flirt, and a damned skillful one, too. With all the necessary equipment. On the other hand, she was a True Believer in her husband and his cause. Before I left her at the Garden on the way home to drop off Spot, she'd spent the whole taxi ride telling me that the real tragedy of her husband's death had been that he wouldn't get to finish his book.

It was to be his magnum opus, the one that was going to return him to his former best-selling glory and influence. The one, she said, that might get the human race on the way to seeing reality instead of its deceptive reflections. As she spoke, her voice was hoarse with frustration that now it would never happen.

It was to have been called "God's Image—Man's Image," and it was planned on a mammoth scale, along the lines of half a million words, of which only the first two chapters, a fifty-thousand-word overview, and about forty thousand words on religious symbolism, had been finished. I said that that much could probably be published, and she agreed, but it was small consolation. He had been so wrapped up in the project; he'd been putting his thoughts in order for more than three years now . . .

And that was about where we were when we'd gotten to the Garden.

I thought about it some more, shaking my head. I supposed it wasn't out of the question for a woman to be an incredible come-on artist at the same time she played Saint Paul to her husband's Christ, but I had a hard time making it add up. And if she had been faking either of those two roles tonight, Carla Dinkover was more than a good actress, she was downright dangerous.

I was still puzzling over it when a voice said, "Mr. Cobb?"

I looked up to see Bea Dunney. "What are you doing here?" she said.

I grinned at her. "Freezing," I said.

"I would guess so, standing here in the cold with no gloves on."

I stuck my hands deeper in my pocket and made a mental note to replace the gloves I'd ruined with blood at Harris's place. Which reminded me, I'd have to check up on Harris tonight, maybe go see him at the hospital tomorrow.

"You have a point," I conceded. "I saw you skate tonight; I was very impressed."

She smiled. "Thank you. It's nice to be recognized. It used to be I was the only one who knew I was a good skater. I'm glad Max got me this featured spot."

"Max Brother? He's your agent, too?"

"Sure. How do you think I got to appear on Wendy's show? All one big happy family. Today TV, tomorrow the world, right?"

I used to think that. "Where's Wendy?" I asked.

"Waiting for her?"

"No, I'm going to a Christmas pageant as an icicle, and I'm rehearsing. Yes, Bea, I'm waiting for her."

"She's in the Jacuzzi. Her knee, you know. Fragile. I've been lucky that way. All these years, and nothing worse than a sore ass."

Considering I was freezing to death, I was enjoying the conversation. If you're going to freeze, you might as well do it in the company of a pretty girl, I suppose. Bea, for some reason, was really enjoying it. She was teasing me, but not in the way Carla Dinkover had. It was as if Bea had some secret she was trying to lead me to.

"All how many years?" I asked. I figured I might as well play along.

"Same as Wendy, just about. We used to skate against each other sometimes at state youth championships. Do you know who the last person to beat Wendy in competition was?"

"I'll take a wild backhand stab at it," I said. "You?"

"How smart you are! Yes, me. Sports trivia. We were seventeen or so. Just before I turned pro."

"Why?"

"Why what?" She knew why what, she just wanted me to say it.

"Why didn't you keep competing? It might have been you with the gold medal."

A blue flame is very hot. I thought that when I saw her eyes.

"It's nice of you to say so," she said, but her tone said, you'd better believe it. "But life isn't fair, you know? It costs a lot to be a world class skater, Matt. Is it okay to call you Matt?"

"I called you Bea."

"Okay. The first thing you have to do is go live in Colorado, where all the coaches are. Then you have to *pay* a coach. Do you want to know how much Wendy has paid Danov over the last ten years or so? Unbelievable.

"Wendy's father was a hotshot college professor, and her stepmother has family money, so no problem. My father owned a bakery, my mother is a secretary in a bank. They were just about able, with every-thing mortgaged, to keep me going. Then my father died, and Mom couldn't do it alone. So, when I got the chance to make some money skating, I took it."

"Couldn't you have found someone to sponsor you?"

"Maybe. I was mixed up—I probably should have. There's more money on the other side of an Olympic medal than I've ever been close to. Still, things change, don't they? They're changing for me. My big turn is coming soon." She went on in a similar vein for a few minutes without saying anything specific. Finally she asked me what time it was. I told her, but she didn't believe me because I didn't look at my watch.

I took my hand out of my pocket (reluctantly), let her take a look, then shoved the hand back home.

"How did you do that?"

"I don't know," I said, and she didn't believe that either.

She said she had to go, waved me a cheery good-bye with a mittened hand, then stepped into Seventh Avenue. I noticed without thinking much about it that she didn't go across the street to the Statler but got into a cab which took her away through the now slightly thinner traffic.

It was only a few seconds later that Wendy appeared, wearing much the same motley outfit she'd had on this afternoon, and she was carry-ing a battered gym bag. It was hard to reconcile this look with that of the silk-sheathed goddess I'd seen inside.

As Wendy walked toward me, I could see she was favoring her right leg a little.

Wendy smiled and said hi.

"Hi. Does it hurt much?"

"Wow," she said, "is it that noticeable?"

"Only to an ex-jock," I told her. "I've done my share of walking funny."

"It's okay. These two shows a day, plus the extra stuff for the TV show is a lot of wear and tear. It's nothing a Jacuzzi and a wipe with DMSO won't help."

"If I'd known you were going to spend some time in the tub, I could have stayed and watched the finale."

"I'm sorry, Matt. I should have put it in the note."

"You didn't even know if I was going to be here, no big deal. But why did you want to see me? Is something wrong?"

"Nothing *new.*"

"That's what I meant."

"No. When I got here, I was thinking how nice it was of you to buy me lunch."

"The Network bought you lunch."

"You took me. I thought I'd buy you dinner. I thought that if you made it to the show, you wouldn't have had a chance to eat, right?"

"I had a few peanuts at a bar. You don't have to do this, you know."

"I want to." She lowered her eyes. "After a performance, you know, with the people cheering for me and everything, going back to a hotel room alone is the pits. Such a letdown."

"Where's Mrs. Speir?"

"Schenectady. She's got a cousin up there—that's really why she's back east. She just spent a couple of days with me because the show happened to be here. Just her luck to be there when it happened. The police said it was okay for her to go."

I nodded. Despite all the grim warnings you see on TV about not leaving town, police are usually very polite about that sort of thing, especially if you aren't planning to cross any state lines. I wondered, though, how they'd feel if they heard Carla Dinkover's allegation that Mrs. Speir and the late doctor had been lovers long ago. I wondered if Wendy knew it, but decided this wasn't the time to ask.

"I would love to go to dinner with you," I said.

"Great!"

"*But.*" Wendy's face fell and I felt like a louse. "I really have to get home and walk Spot and feed him. I've been terrible to him the last couple of days."

"Well, where do you live?"

"Central Park West. In the Sixties. Does that mean anything to you?"

"No. Except I think that's where Dinkover lived." She shivered when she mentioned his name, thought I admit it might have been the wind. "Don't they have restaurants in that neighborhood?"

"They have restaurants *everywhere* in New York."

"Okay. I wouldn't mind seeing Spot again. I'll take you out after you walk him. Sound acceptable?"

"Better," I said. "I was hoping you'd think of it."

She returned my smile and hooked her arm in mine as we walked off to get a cab.

CHAPTER TEN

Spot, well exercised and well fed, was sleeping contentedly on the white rug back at the Sloan's apartment. Wendy and I sat at opposite ends of the big leather couch, talking.

We were also well exercised and well fed, having eaten chicken and ribs at the Swiss Chalet Bar-B-Que on Seventy-second Street. Wendy, at her own insistence, had paid. Cash, no less. Then we'd come back here.

We talked about all sorts of things. Team sports versus individual sports. The relative merits of places we'd been. Movies—being on the road in strange towns all the time led Wendy to see a lot of movies.

"Bea Dunney's going to be in a movie, you know," she said. "Max suggested her for the part."

"She mentioned he was her agent," I said.

Wendy was wearing a yellow and purple Los Angeles Kings hockey jersey tonight, size extra-extra small. The Kings had had one made specially for her after she joined them in some kind of fund-raising show. She reached inside the neck and pulled out the tie strings. She fiddled with them as we talked.

"He wasn't her agent before the movie came up, actually," she said. "He heard that they needed somebody who could skate for the part, so he went out and signed her up."

"I thought he already handled somebody who could skate."

She looked up from the strings with a kind of crooked smile. "They wanted somebody who could skate who could play June Lockhart's daughter. Somebody obviously ethnic would 'affect the dynamics of the relationships.' "

"They talk like that a lot," I said. "I hate to say it, but it could even be true."

"Oh, I know. They'd have to explain me, that I was adopted, or something like that, and there's a lot of other crap like if they gave me a boyfriend or something, the fact that I'm Japanese would be an element. I know all that. Still . . ."

"It would be nice to be a movie star. It's hard work, you know."

"I'm used to hard work, believe me. But if I could do movies, I'd work a couple of months, then flake out the rest of the year. I'm getting sick and tired of touring. I think I told you that this afternoon."

"You mentioned it. Do you like jellybeans?"

She looked at me and laughed. "Jellybeans? Doesn't everybody?"

"What color?"

"You're serious, aren't you? The black ones. I love licorice."

I got up and went to the kitchen to check the jellybean supply. "You're in luck," I called back to her. I got a couple of Steuben Glass candy dishes (the Sloans buy nothing but the best), and filled them with jellybeans, black for her, purple for me.

I put her dish on the coffee table in front of her. "I don't believe this," she said. "Most guys have etchings."

"I just have a terminal sweet tooth. My dentist loves me for it."

"I'll bet he does," she said. She popped a jellybean between her lips.

"I just realized I was being a lousy host. And I wanted some jellybeans for myself. Can I get you something to drink?"

"What goes with black jellybeans, for God's sake?"

I suggested anisette.

"You're crazy, do you know that?"

"That seems to be the consensus."

"Nothing to drink for now," she said. "Thank you all the same. Where were we?"

"Bea Dunney's movie. How you understood why your agent hadn't tried to get you the part."

"Oh, right. I wasn't overjoyed, but I guess I understood. My stepmother sure didn't, though."

I attempted to say "Aha" at the same moment I tried to swallow some grape-flavored goo. I don't recommend it. I made a horrible noise getting my throat cleared.

Wendy crossed the couch in a single bound, concern showing on her face. "Are you all right?" she demanded.

"I'm fine," I said. "That just tied up with something I heard earlier."

"Something important?" Wendy's face was eager.

"Probably not," I said. "It's just the first time *anything* has made any sense since Dinkover showed up at the Network yesterday afternoon."

"What makes sense, Matt?"

"Did your stepmother confront Brother about this? In public?"

Wendy made a face. "Yes, she did. Embarrassing, isn't it? This was *supposed* to have been kept quiet, though. How did you hear about it?"

I told her about my meeting with the widow Dinkover.

"Her," Wendy said. No further comment was necessary. "What did she want from you? Besides the obvious, I mean."

"She wanted to know which of you five people at the rink let Dinkover in."

"Her and the police," Wendy said. She leaned back against the couch and closed her eyes. "I don't think I can stand this, Matt. Things are worse with him dead. Now she's going to torment me in his name."

"Nobody's going to torment you if we can get this thing cleared up."

"What's that supposed to mean? Do you think I let him in? Or Helena or Max or Bea or Alex?"

That wasn't rhetoric. Wendy's dark eyes watched me intently, wanting me to say no.

Instead, I said, "Maybe." Wendy groaned. "Look," I went on, "last night I was ready to believe somebody had mugged Harris Brophy to get the magnetic key to the Blades Club. The theory was that the killer wanted to get at you or one of your party, and Dinkover somehow got in his way."

"By coincidence? Why couldn't the killer have wanted to kill Dinkover?"

"How did he know he was going to be there? Sure, he could have lured Dinkover there to kill him—a phone call saying he could have another shot at convincing you would have brought the old man running, if I'm any judge.

"But why should the killer bother? All he had to do was get Dinkover out of the house, and he could handle him the way he (in this theory) handled Harris."

"Maybe he wanted to frame me for it," Wendy said. "Everybody knows I hated him."

I shook my head. "He couldn't be sure you didn't have an alibi."

"I don't, though," Wendy said. "You were there when we talked to Lieutenant Martin. Each of us was alone at one time or another during the important time."

I picked up a handful of jellybeans. Wendy told me to be careful, and I smiled at her as I put a couple in my mouth. I was stumped by the same problem that had always stumped me. Why the Blades Club? It could be that the killer just hoped the intrigue surrounding Wendy and her entourage would give the police enough to keep them busy. But what about Harris's apartment, then? That was consistent with a professional mugger/burglar, less so with a killer. Unless the killer had been very smooth, and had covered his tracks that way.

It boiled down to two rival theories:

One—Harris had been mugged, and his keys taken, to get access to the Blades Club; while there, the mugger had killed Dinkover. Intentionally? Perhaps, but that caused complications. If not intentionally, what *had* our friend intended to do? Who was the real target?

Two—the mugging of Harris was one of those unfortunate things that can happen to any New Yorker, like a power failure or your subway going out of service. Paul Dinkover had been given entry, then killed by one of the five people present last night. If so, who? And why? Wendy had hated Dinkover and made no bones about it. But unless she was actually insane (which, in my admittedly untrained opinion, she was not), she had too much to lose by doing him in at that time in that place. That held true for all of them, in one way or another, even if they did have motives against Dinkover. Not that any of them seemed to. The only one I could see doing something like that was Danov, and, as Wendy had said, he wasn't crazy, only Russian.

And of course, the one we keep coming back to, no matter which theory we like: *What in the name of all the saints did Dinkover expect to accomplish by crawling to the flag?*

"Matt?" Wendy's voice was soft. "I don't know what you're thinking, but if you keep making that face, you're going to give yourself a headache."

I smiled at her. "You're right," I said. "How's this?"

"Lots better. What were you thinking about?"

"Ramifications. I do that all the time."

"Think about ramifications of murders?"

"Not murders all the time, thank God. Most of the time, not even crimes." I decided it might be a good idea to change the subject.

"There's one thing I have to say to you, Wendy. I should have said it before."

She raised an eyebrow. "Oh?"

"You were magnificent out there on the ice. Absolutely breathtaking."

"Matt, don't," she said. You might have thought I told her she stank.

"What's the matter? I mean it. I'm not the sort to toss superlatives around, you know. It's rare for somebody to be truly great at anything. It's rare even to meet someone who is. That's all I want to tell you. I'm not trying to butter you up or anything."

She mumbled something; I asked her to speak up.

"There's more to me than skating!" she yelled. Spot woke up, gave her a dirty look, licked his chops, and settled back to sleep.

Wendy was quieter but no less intense. "I'm so *tired* of this. I'm not *real* to anybody. I'm some sort of athletic genius—Howard Cosell called me that—or I'm America's Little Oriental Sweetheart. I'm afraid to smoke in public, or say what I think, or date, or anything because of my image.

"That's all I am, you know. Really. To Max Brother, I'm an image he can market. To my stepmother, I'm a Duty, and maybe a souvenir of my father. To Danov, I'm some kind of puppet—he really thinks he does all the work. If you asked him, he'd tell you the relationship between a coach and a skater is exactly like the one between an architect and a bricklayer.

"And to Dinkover, I was nothing; a mixed-up tragedy to be blamed on my father." Her eyes were big and moist. "Maybe I hated him because I'm afraid he's right."

"Wendy, stop it," I said.

She shook her head, angry at the interruption. "No, dammit! Do you know the only time I feel real is when I'm *skating?* That's the only time I feel sure of myself, the only time I know what the hell I'm supposed to do!"

She made a fist and chewed on one of the knuckles. "Then here you are. You told me jokes and made me laugh. You listened to my troubles. You got Dinkover off my back, at least for a while. *And in all this time, you never mentioned skating once!*

"I said to myself, 'He doesn't *care!* He'd like me even if I weren't famous or rich.' " She looked at her lap. "I—I've been falling in love with you, if you haven't been too stupid to notice."

"Wow," I said, or something equally apt.

"Then you come up with *this* bullshit, about 'truly magnificent,' and 'absolutely breathtaking.' What am I supposed to do now? Say thank you and sign your autograph book?"

She went back to her knuckle. I sat there feeling stupid. Finally, I took a breath and began to talk.

"Wendy," I said. "I'm not going to say you overreacted—"

"Gee, thanks."

"—because you probably didn't. After all my talk about ramifications, I have to admit I didn't think of the ramifications of saying what I said to you.

"I only said you were a great skater because I could see it was true and because in a dumb sort of way I meant to thank you for showing it to me. Most people, most of us everyday mediocrities, don't know how to deal with a genius."

"For God's sake, Matt, don't make it worse."

"Let me finish. I met Oscar Robertson once. My idol. The greatest guard who ever played basketball. I couldn't think of a goddam word to say to him. I wanted to tell him what he'd meant to me, how it was my greatest ambition to *be him.* I never opened my mouth because I was afraid he'd laugh at me. He probably wouldn't have; that's not the point. It was just that his greatness was so obvious to me that—Hell,

I'm not saying this very well. Fifteen years later, and I'm still tongue-tied.

"Robertson deserved to hear me say that, him and all the other famous strangers who affected me, changed my life, really, that I was too lazy to write to, or too shy to talk to.

"What you did on the ice tonight, and what you did in the Olympics, affected me the same way. But I *never could have told you* if you weren't real to me. A person. A friend. I could finally get it out and let the one time stand for all the others."

"Come off it," Wendy said. "You meet famous people all the time."

"Sure. Damn few geniuses, though." I reached across the couch and took her hand. "Look, Wendy, from what you've told me, you've worked hard all your life to be great. I wanted to let you know that you succeeded. That's all."

She was silent, but she didn't take her hand away.

"Another thing," I said. "I saw you skate about nine o'clock. I met you outside about twenty to ten. It's twelve thirty now. That means for two and a half hours, I went on treating you like a person, while I was getting up the guts to tell you how good you are. A genius is still a person, and I intend to go on treating you like one."

Wendy looked at me for a long time. "I think you mean it," she said at last.

"Cross my heart."

"You could do something a lot better," she said, "than treat me like a person."

"What's that?"

"Treat me like a woman."

And suddenly she was in my arms, and her hands were clenched in my hair, and her lips were on mine, hot and sweet. When the kiss ended we looked at each other, and her almond eyes were very warm, very wise. We kissed again, more slowly. I took her to the bedroom. Soon the jeans were gone and the hockey jersey was gone (the strings had already been untied, after all). I felt strong muscles beneath smooth brown skin and spent the night making love to a genius. Who happened to be a real person.

A real woman.

Sometime in the night, Wendy rolled over and gasped.

"What's the matter?" I demanded.

"Nothing. Just my stupid knee. Skating, walking, making love—too much strenuous activity for one day."

"I didn't want to hurt you."

"Shut up," she said. She craned her neck back and kissed the tip of my nose. "It was worth it. Where's my bag?"

"In the living room." She rose from the bed and limped off toward the living room. I watched her go, sorry she was in pain, but glad she was here.

I yawned and decided I might as well go to the bathroom. Wendy was there already. She was wearing the jersey again, and she had one shapely leg propped up on the rim of the tub. She had a jar in her left hand and a piece of cotton in her right. She dipped the cotton in the jar, and it came away stained brownish yellow.

"Hello," she said. She rubbed the cotton over her knee. There was wetness on her skin for about a second; then it looked as if she had never put anything on at all.

"That is fast," I said.

"Don't kiss me," she said, reading my mind. "My mouth tastes disgusting. Uck. Do you have any Listerine?"

"In the cabinet."

"Good. Only thing that kills the taste." She stretched out her leg, bent it a few times, then reapplied the DMSO. She stretched again. "That's better. Now let me gargle."

I kissed the back of her neck, making her giggle, then I went off to use the other bathroom. Wendy rejoined me a few minutes later.

"Safe to kiss you?" I asked. She showed me it was.

"Wendy," I said, "I want you to be careful."

"With the knee? I'm used to it."

"Not just with the knee. There's too much going on and too little of it is understood. I'm going to have my people hanging around you when you go anywhere."

"You will, huh? What about you?"

"I'll be there whenever I can. Maybe I'll catch you in the finale this afternoon."

"Don't overdo it. I don't want you to get bored, you know."

"No chance," I told her.

"Okay, then. Let me show you how to do this without hurting my knee . . ."

"Read label directions carefully; do not exceed recommended dosage."
—Standard disclaimer, TV drug advertising

CHAPTER ELEVEN

I had to go see Tom Falzet in the morning, so I called Al St. John and had him take Wendy wherever she had to go. I checked with Wendy first, of course, but she seemed to be in a mood to give her image a kick in the behind and therefore didn't care who knew we'd spent the night together. If Al thought anything of it, it didn't show on his face. Since he'd be at the Garden, anyway, I gave him an extra key to the Network room and told him to check on progress there.

The president's office is the entire thirty-seventh floor of the Tower of Babble, the kind of place Dick Powell used to have in the fantasy numbers of old Busby Berkeley musicals, with conference tables, and steps, and plateaus you have to cross before gaining the Presence. All of which, as far as I can see, having no purpose other than to impress the visitor with his own insignificance.

The room hadn't been designed with Falzet in mind, but he had made it his own. This was a man who had raised pomposity to a Fine Art.

Falzet was tall, with gray hair and the kind of toothy, long-nosed good looks that always remind me of Old Money. He could be charming when he wanted to; I had seen him do it. He had yet to be charming to me.

"Where were you yesterday?" he demanded. No hello.

I took a chair, crossed my legs, and spent plenty of time adjusting my pants. "It *is* a lovely morning, isn't it? Do you think we'll have snow for Christmas?"

"If you were where you deserve to be," he said, "you'd *never* see snow. I wanted to see you yesterday, Cobb. Correct me if I'm wrong, but I think I *am* still running this Network."

This boded well; Falzet was always easiest to handle when he tried to be funny.

"Well, sir, if you'll wait a second, I'll call Dun and Bradstreet to check."

"Never mind! The Network has been receiving unfavorable publicity."

"Yes sir."

"It's not even the Network's fault!"

"Not even a little bit, sir."

"That crazy old man had no business there. That was a Network facility and should have been secure."

"Not much we can do if someone let him in. Especially if that someone, a business associate of the Network or someone close to a business associate of the Network, let him in expressly to kill him."

"One of your people should have been there!"

"My person who should have been there was in the hospital fighting for his life. Shall I send him flowers in your name?"

Falzet was impervious to cracks like that. "I want you to get to the bottom of this, Cobb. I want this business cleared up and out of the media. With the killer caught, if possible."

"Thank you, sir, for your guidance. Now I know what to do. I was all at sea, before." I really had to wonder why Falzet ever wanted to see me. All we ever did was get on each other's nerves.

This time came close to setting a record. I managed to get out of the office with no blood being shed, but it was a near thing.

The next stop was Network News on the sixth floor, where I paid a visit to Bill Bevacqua. Bill is the Network News librarian, charged with keeping track of all the film and videotape (miles of it) that we use in our news operations.

I found him filing updated obituaries. That's something he and the rest of the News department have to attend to every now and then. When somebody attains prominence, they put together a bio for him.

If you attain *real* prominence, your story gets narrated by the Anchorman himself. Anyway, the Network has these things ready; all we have to do is wait for you to die. If you've ever wondered how the Network was able to whip a half-hour special about Elvis Presley on the air within an hour and twenty minutes of the time he kicked off, now you know.

Bill is a slight, good-humored guy who gets lonely among the cans of three-quarter-inch videotape. He looked up from his list and smiled over his glasses.

"Matthew! What can I do for you?"

"I didn't get to see the Dinkover obit—do you still have it?"

"You didn't get here a moment too soon—it was going in the histori-cal section in about ten minutes. Hold on a second." He punched a few buttons on a computer terminal, made a few notes on a piece of paper, and muttered, "Okay, you people live for a while, will you? I'm tired of rearranging obits."

He turned back to me. "You want the obit piece or the whole file on him?"

"The whole thing, Bill, if you can."

"Sure. How's it going?" I grunted; he laughed. "I've got confidence in you. Maybe you'll find something in my tapes. If you want to check out everybody, I've got some great stuff of Wendy Ichimi."

I told him I'd pass on Wendy's tapes for now. I already knew more about her than any video tape could tell me. Bill got on the phone and called for an engineer to run the tapes for me. In all the time I've worked for the Network, I have never touched a videotape machine. TV is a strongly unionized industry.

I was just as glad, after I'd watched a few tapes, that I didn't have anything expensive within reach, because I probably would have broken it in frustration.

It wasn't that I didn't learn *anything*. I learned that Dinkover had a tendency to repeat himself over the years, using the same insults for Johnson, Nixon, and Ford. I learned what a pitiful bunch the Landover Four were. Stern faces, defiant, justified in taking a life here because of what Nixon was doing there. But deep in their eyes, fear.

In a way, a TV camera is like an X-ray machine. It takes time, but it works. Joseph McCarthy used TV as a weapon to build his power, but the senator found the blade turning in his hands. He overexposed himself, and finally, destroyed himself. Just by letting TV cameras stay pointed at his face too long.

The Landover Four didn't get as much exposure as McCarthy did, but they got enough for me to see they were indeed dancing for Dr. Dinkover. It occurred to me that it might be worthwhile to check with the police to see if Velda Delinski, June Lathen, or Cyril Guzick were still in jail. John Free, more or less the ringleader of the Four, was dead and therefore out of it. I hoped. Things were weird enough without resurrections or ghosts to deal with.

I looked at the tapes twice. Neither Dinkover, nor any of his friends or enemies, not even the Anchorman, mentioned anything about eagles. I thanked Bill and the engineer more from politeness than gratitude, then left.

My next stop was the hospital. Harris Brophy was still in intensive care, and it took some doing for me to get in to see him. In the end, I had to have someone call my friend Cernak so he could vouch for me. I wound up owing Cernak the plot for the next month of "Agony of Love" in return, and I made a note of his home phone number so I could fill him in.

The nurse outside told me Harris was getting better, but to me he looked dead. The only evidence for his continued existence was the regular jumping of the line on the heart monitor and the fact that Shirley Arnstein wasn't thrown across Harris's form, crying.

Shirley wasn't, in fact, there at all.

"I made her go home," Harris said. It was a monotone croak, issued from the corner of his mouth. "High time you got here, Matt."

"How long have you been conscious?"

" 'Bout an hour and a half. I figured you'd be here waiting for my eyelids to flutter." He raised a hand in the direction of his eyelids. They did more than flutter, his eyes popped out like Ping-Pong balls.

"Jesus Christ, that hurts!" he said. "I think I liked it better unconscious." His eyes drooped nearly closed again.

"You were almost permanently unconscious."

"I know, I know. Shirley nearly worked herself up into hysterics telling me about it. She hadn't had any sleep for two days. Nurse told me they couldn't get her out of here. I made her go home and get some rest. I told her I wasn't going anywhere." Harris tried to laugh, but from the corner of his mouth the best he could manage was a feeble "heh, heh."

I told him he sounded like somebody from an old Warner Brothers gangster picture.

"Right down . . . right down to getting rubbed out on a street corner?"

"Are they giving you anything for pain?" I didn't like the effort it cost him to talk.

"I'm flying, Matt. This is just major league pain. It's the knee that hurts the most. Did you know the son of a bitch broke my knee?"

"I knew it. Have the cops spoken to you yet?"

"No. Shirley wants to be here when they do, so she's going to call them . . . call them when she wakes up. Taking care of her little Harris. She's a great kid. Great kid."

A nurse came by and gave Harris a pill and me a dirty look. She'd already told me not to tire him out. I nodded at her and got down to business.

"Harris, did you see who did this?"

Harris looked up at the ceiling and sighed. "No, goddammit," he said at last. "I didn't see anything, or . . . or hear anything. I got to the bottom of the stoop . . . turned to walk uptown, to get a cab to meet those people at the . . . the hotel, and that's the last thing I remember until this morning. I'm sorry . . . feel so stupid . . . supposed to be a pro . . ."

Harris was drifting off, and I was willing to let him go, since I'd learned what I wanted to know, or rather, found out I *wasn't* going to learn what I wanted to know. Still, as long as I was there, I thought I'd try one more thing.

"Harris," I said. He was still going on about how stupid he felt. "Harris, cut that stuff out and listen to me for a second. What could an eagle mean?"

I figured this was the kind of question it might be best to put to someone well on his way to medicine-induced slumber. And by God, Harris had an answer for me.

"Gold," he said.

"That's right, the eagle was gold." I wondered how he knew about it.

Shirley was dedicated to her work, all right, but I didn't think she'd use Harris's first moments of consciousness bringing him up to date on the case.

"U.S. currency," Harris went on, and I stopped wondering. He was talking numismatics, not murder. "Ten-dollar gold piece. Five dollars . . . half eagle. Twenty . . . double eagle . . . pretty coins . . . always wanted to get hold of some . . ."

I figured that was a healthier topic for him to dwell on as he went to sleep than his own shortcomings. I also wondered how he would take it when he learned his coin collection had been stolen.

I whispered a good-bye to him, as my beeper went off. I went to the nearest pay phone and checked in. My secretary told me Al St. John had reported in; something had happened, and I was to meet him at the Garden for a full report.

It was turning out to be one of those days. Al met me in the Network control-room-in-progress, and we talked amid the curses of the technicians in whose way we always seemed to be.

"There was a mess at Brother's office," Al said.

"It figures. What happened?"

"Good Lord! What didn't happen? For one thing, Miss Ichimi's mother returned from upstate and tried to fire Max Brother as Miss Ichimi's agent."

"Stepmother," I said.

"Of course. Sorry. Anyway, she was there when I arrived with Miss Ichimi. I wanted to wait in the outer office or something, but they all wanted me to stay."

"All? Who constituted all?"

"I was getting to that. Miss Ichimi—she seemed to see me as your deputy, and she wanted me to be around for that reason." Al cleared his throat. "Matt, let me know if I'm out of line about this, but is there anything I should know about you and Miss Ichimi?"

I grinned at him. "Just that a good executive sometimes can't help getting involved with his work." I felt the grin fade. "But she's been tense over the whole situation. How did she take this latest noise?"

"She was furious with her mother—stepmother. Told her to mind her own business."

"Who else was there?"

"Danov. Then Carla Dinkover showed up."

"What?"

"Stormed right past the receptionist, said she had an appointment. Claimed Brother had called her and asked her to come. He supposedly had something to tell her."

To hear Al tell it, there had been quite a scene. I was glad I missed it. Wendy had been near hysterics and had stormed out, leaving a bunch of angry and bewildered people behind her. A check back with Brother's office reassured him the incident had blown over, but he still thought I ought to know about it.

"Thanks," I said. I remembered Shirley's advice and told him what a good job I thought he was doing.

"What should I do now?"

"Didn't you work the graveyard shift last night? Then come right from the Tower to my place?"

"Yes."

"Well, take the rest of the day off, for God's sake. I'm going to want you around this ice skating business whenever I can't be there. I'll call you tonight or tomorrow morning to tell you where I want you. Does that sound all right?"

"Sure," he said. "Good Lord, I've been hoping for more responsibility, all along. I know you depend on Harris and Shirley, and I'm sorry this had to happen . . ."

"But you're glad for the opportunity. I understand. Just one thing, Al."

"What's that?"

"Don't forget to carry your beeper." No smile from him. I went on before he could tell me he *always* carried his beeper, and I had to explain it was a joke. "Where's Wendy?"

"In her dressing room, with a Garden security guard outside. I had to convince her it was a good idea. Even at that, she stood outside on the street for ten minutes, signing autographs. I almost had to pull her away."

"I'll talk to her. Now you get out of here."

Before heading down to Wendy's dressing room, I stepped into the arena to take a look at the show (it was Bea Dunney in the melodrama again) and to think about that business in Brother's office.

What the hell had been going on with Mrs. Dinkover? If she dreamed up that plan herself, she should be ashamed of herself. What could she have expected to accomplish, besides getting people upset? The only person who seemed to benefit by the whole thing was Brother, whose firing (if firing there was to be; I'd have to ask Wendy about that) had been delayed by the distraction. But if he had really made that phone call, he was playing a real long shot. What if Mrs. Dinkover didn't show up? What if her arrival hadn't worked?

No, what it looked like was someone out to make trouble for Mrs. Dinkover and for Wendy and company. Somebody very good at it, too.

There was a noise from the crowd that made me look up, something between a gasp and a moan. It's the universal cry of concern from that collective being a sports audience becomes. It means something has happened to one of the athletes.

Bea Dunney was sitting on the ice, legs splayed ungracefully before her. She was supporting herself with her hands and shaking her head. It really *was* one of those days. I walked over to the nearest spectator, a young mother with two kids, and asked her what happened.

"She spilled grape drink on herself, that's what happened!" She indicated a little girl about three years old who had a purple mustache and goatee and a broad, irregular purple blotch down the front of her yellow jumper. The mother was dabbing at it ineffectually with a paper towel.

"I swear," she said. "I think they always ask for grape because it makes the worst stain. Do you have a handkerchief? A Wash'n Dri?"

"No, sorry. I meant to ask what happened on the ice."

"With these two, I don't have time to see anything."

The other child, a boy about eight, whose hair and clothes were inhumanly neat for a kid that age, piped up with, "I saw it!"

"Okay, what happened?"

"Didn't you see it?"

"If I saw it, I wouldn't have to ask you, would I?"

"Well, I thought this was like a quiz. To see if I understood, you know?"

"Okay, let's call it a quiz. What happened?"

"Well," the kid began. He sounded exactly like President Reagan. "The villain was holding her over his head. He was going to tie her to the railroad tracks. She was struggling, and he stumbled and then he dropped her. I thought it was part of the show, but Lily got scared and spilled her drink. But I think the lady hurt her leg."

That apparently was the case, because just as the kid finished filling me in, Bea Dunney rose to her skates to the applause of the crowd. She skated in a circle, then again in the other direction, picked up her left leg and rotated the ankle a few times, then nodded to her co-stars, and the show went on. More applause. She seemed okay, so I left the stands and made my way down to Wendy's dressing room.

Wendy was the only person in the Ice-Travaganza to rate a personal dressing room—the other skaters used locker rooms, one for males, the other for females. There was a short route to Wendy's dressing room through the girls' locker room, but I didn't want to abuse my carte blanche. Instead, I took the long way round.

I met the guard at the door (there was a star on it, by the way—Max Brother's idea, Wendy told me later) and told him Miss Ichimi was expecting me. He maintained a just-short-of-hostile skepticism it was a pleasure to see. Everything personal aside, the Network had a big investment in Wendy's well-being.

The guard knocked on the door and announced me. A few seconds later, the door opened, and Wendy took my hand and led me inside. The guard took it all in with big eyes.

"Hello," I said after a welcoming kiss. "Far be it from me to lecture you about your image, but that guard is going to tell people about this."

Wendy was wearing her white outfit but had yet to put on her socks and skates. She twirled around in front of the mirror, making her skirt flare prettily.

"It's all a plan," she said. "I'm changing my image."

"Mmm," I said. "Listen, my dear. What happened last night was wonderful, but I don't think I'm too crazy about the idea of being used as an image warper."

"What do you mean?"

"I mean if the idea behind all this if for you to get it into the gossip columns that you're sleeping with somebody, maybe we ought to move our relationship back to strictly business."

Her dark eyes were puzzled. "How can you say that? Didn't you hear me talk to you last night? I was only joking—God, Matt, I never thought you'd . . ."

There you go, Cobb, I told myself, you've done it again. This relationship was shaping up as a series of misunderstandings.

"All right," I said, "I'm sorry. This time *I* overreacted. It's just that macho mythology to the contrary, guys *do* care why women want to sleep with them."

"I'll keep that in mind. Boy, are you touchy today."

"Preemptive strike," I said.

"What's *that* mean?"

"After the scene in Max Brother's office this morning, I figured you'd be on edge. That made me nervous, and I wound up snapping at you. It seems to have worked," I added. "Neither one of us is climbing a wall at the moment."

"I've decided not to let it get to me," she said.

"That's healthy." I didn't tell her that things have a way of getting to you whether you plan to let them or not.

She seemed to hear it, anyway. "I mean it," she said. "There's no reason I have to be crazy because people around me are. Cautious maybe, but not crazy."

"Good for you," I said, and meant it. Part of Wendy's problem, it seemed to me, was that she had spent too much time taking advice.

"Listen, Wendy, do you know anybody who collects coins?"

"Coins? Why?"

"Specifically United States gold pieces? They were called eagles."

"Oh," she said. "Ohhh. Still chasing that one down, huh?"

"Compulsive," I said.

"I wish I knew what I meant when I said that. You, too, I bet. No, Matt, I don't know anybody who collects that sort of eagle." She shrugged. "Anyway, the more I think about it, the less I think it means. Maybe *I* just have a thing about eag—"

There was a knock on the door. "Miss Dunney," the guard said.

Wendy looked a question at me; I looked ignorance back at her. Wendy shrugged again and said, "Come in, Bea."

The door opened, and Bea Dunney came in, also barefoot, with her skates slung over her shoulder. I remember thinking that if athlete's foot ever got introduced among this gang, it would reach epidemic proportions in no time.

The blond skater was apologetic. "I hope I'm not interrupting anything, Wendy. It's just that I twisted my ankle out there. I guess I jinxed myself yesterday, Matt, when I told you I never got hurt. Anyway, it's not broken or anything, but it hurts, and I'd rather not miss my spot in the finale. I'm going to have Jackie tape it, but first, if it's okay, I'd like to borrow your stuff."

"Stuff?"

"You know. The illegal stuff. DMSO, is it?"

"Oh, sure," Wendy said. "Let me get it for you." Wendy bent over her gym bag (an incredibly sexy cheesecake pose, by the way) and pulled out the brown glass jar.

She held it up to the light and squinted at it. "Sure, go ahead and use it—I've got a lot more left than I thought."

She handed over the jar. Bea said, "Thanks," and "Nice to see you again, Matt," and went to leave. Wendy said, "Wait," and handed her a couple of cotton balls. I reached into my pocket and pulled out the remainder of a roll of Wint-O-Green Life Savers and handed them over, too.

"What are these for?" Bea wanted to know.

"Cover up the taste."

Bea smiled. "Such good friends," she said with friendly sarcasm, and then she was gone.

"She'll talk about us," I told Wendy.

"So she'll talk about us. Big deal. You sound like you're ashamed of me or something."

"I'm not ashamed of you."

"What is it then?"

"I don't know. Maybe I don't think I'm worth blowing your image over."

"To hell with my image! How many times do I have to say that?"

"Also, you're very young."

"I'm what? Eight years younger than you are?"

"Something like that."

"Matt, that's nothing. Look, I'm free, yellow, and twenty-one, and I make my own decisions, all right?"

"Very funny," I said. "But yes, message received."

"Good," Wendy said. "Besides, if she says too much about us, I can tell people a lot about her and Max Brother."

I raised a brow. "Oh? I saw her taking off somewhere last night. Did this get started before or after the movie part came up?"

Wendy shrugged, then looked at the clock. "I've got to get ready," she said and began to pull on her socks. I asked her how her knee was.

"Fine, so far. You learn fast. And well. I haven't even had to use the DMSO again."

"You're a good teacher. You make learning fun."

She smiled. "I do my best." The smile turned into a puzzled frown. "It's funny, though," Wendy said. "Last night at your place, when I did my knee, I could have sworn that the jar of DMSO was more than half empty."

It occurred to me that Wendy was a pessimist; an optimist would have said "almost half full."

"But when I gave it to Bea," Wendy went on, "it was almost filled up. I have to get my eyes checked or something. Did you ever see anyone skate from ice level?" Wendy asked.

"No, I haven't," I said. It took me a few seconds to answer; my brain was flashing a big sign that said, STANDBY. It had noticed something my consciousness hadn't caught up with yet.

"Come with me out to the ice; I'll tell the show manager, he'll let you stand there. It's interesting. You can tell a lot more from there. How high we get on jumps. How well we hold an edge. In competitions, the judges always sit at ice level. Are you listening to me?"

"The judges sit at ice level," I mumbled. "Of course I'm listening."

"You don't act like it. What's the matter, Matt?"

My subconscious finally let my brain in on the secret. Jar—last night, half empty. Today almost full. Had someone filled it up? If so, with what? More DMSO? Or . . .

"Matt!" Wendy told my back. I paid her no attention. I pulled the door open. The guard tried to stop me, adding a rhetorical "What the hell?" to the proceedings, but I planted the heel of my hand on his sternum and pushed him aside like another door. I sprinted for the girls' locker room.

Naked women, all of them pretty, started to scream as soon as I dashed inside, but it wasn't my arrival that set them off. I looked across the room and saw the reason for the screaming. Bea Dunney, still in the gingham jumper and pigtails she wore as the Innocent Heroine, was lying on the floor, twitching. All around her was a pool of clear liquid, with shards of brown glass in it. Her bare feet and legs sat in the liquid, drinking it in. The air was full of the garlic-and-oyster odor of DMSO.

I set my jaw. I tend to do that when I'm trying to talk myself into shooting craps with my own life. Carefully, I walked around to Bea's head, reached down, and hoping the liquid hadn't spread this far, went to take her under the shoulders.

"Don't touch her!" The guard had his gun out. He pointed it at me. I froze.

Bea Dunney stopped twitching. Her lips and fingernails were blue.

I thought, to hell with it, pulled her back from the pool, then stood with my hands raised. Until Wendy came running up, still barefoot.

"Get the hell out of here!" I barked. "Call the cops. Lieutenant Martin."

The guard scowled at me; I was stealing his lines. I told Wendy to ask for an ambulance, too, but one look at the staring eyes of the girl on the floor told me it would only be a gesture.

"I've got a problem. Believe me, I've got a problem."
—Charles Farrell, *My Little Margie* (CBS)

CHAPTER TWELVE

"I don't *know* what the killer mixed with the DMSO," I told the Frying Nun for about the fiftieth time. "In a Dick Francis book, they mixed it with some horse tranquilizers."

"Figures," Rivetz said. He once told me he reads about one mystery a year. He likes to get mad at them.

Lieutenant Martin was holding his temper. You have to know him a long time before you can tell he's doing that; his brown face gets just a slight touch of purple to it, from all the blood rushing to his head.

"Cobb's not a chemist, Miss Goosens," he said. "Why don't we just wait for what the Medical Examiner has to say?"

The implied message was, everyone should do his (or more to the point, *her)* own job and not try to horn in on others. ADA Goosens got the message, all right. Her acknowledgment took the form of a slit-eyed smile that was off the top end of the smugness scale. For a second it looked as if the lieutenant was toying with the idea of smacking her one, but he thought better of it, and mumbled something under his breath.

"Mr. Cobb may not be a chemist," the Frying Nun intoned, "but he has a disturbing knack for finding corpses. At least this time he has had the good grace to present us with a theory to go along with the young woman's body. I was merely asking him to elaborate."

We were in the Network office-turned-studio, which I had donated to the officials involved to use as a headquarters. Wendy was downstairs, being hysterical all over her stepmother and/or Ivan Danov. All three were under orders not to leave the building.

Typically, Livia Goosens was the only person in the room standing up, and she stood as if she had a poker sewn into the back of her suit. Lieutenant Martin had a swivel chair; I was leaning up against a desk. I had an embarrassing moment when I first went to it—I leaned too hard and sent it sliding backward along the carpeting. I had a near miss at another even more embarrassing moment when I stopped Rivetz inches away from sitting on a fifty-seven-thousand-dollar video switcher.

There was an odd air of quiet in the building. You might not be aware of the noise a crowd makes in the arena, but the whole building changes when they're gone. In this case, they must have gone away puzzled. In the Great Tradition of Show Biz, the Show Went On, but it went on without its star; without Bea Dunney; without, in fact, any more female skaters than those who had been on the ice when Bea keeled over. It must have made for an extremely lopsided finale.

I sighed. "I don't mind elaborating," I said to Livia Goosens, "but I get damned weary of repeating myself."

"Oh, Mr. Cobb," she said coldly. "Indulge me, won't you? You work so well with official investigations."

"Well, since you put it that way, how can I refuse?" I went on to tell her about DMSO; how its pain-relieving properties were almost incidental; how it will dissolve practically anything; how it will carry whatever is dissolved in it right through the skin into the bloodstream. It was the same stuff I'd told Wendy in the restaurant; the same stuff I'd told Livia Goosens herself at least six times already.

"Yes, Mr. Cobb. Quite educational. But what I am interested in is not how this chemical—"

"Dimethylsulfoxide," I interrupted. Once I get started reciting, it's hard to stop.

"Yes. I'm not interested in how the dimethylsulfoxide got the poison into the victim. I am interested in how the poison got into the bottle of dimethylsulfoxide."

"The killer had his own bottle with the poison mixed in. The stuff is easy enough to get—I think somebody at the Network told Wendy a drugstore where she could get it near her hotel. The killer just switched his bottle with the one in Wendy's bag."

"Yes, Mr. Cobb. And when did that happen?"

"After 3 A.M.," I said. "Wendy used it then, and it was fine."

"She told you this?"

"I saw her use it." There goes the image for real now, I thought.

Lieutenant Martin made a face. He's a prude. Under different circumstances he would have made a remark, but not in front of the Frying Nun.

"Actually," I went on, "it had to be after 10 A.M. or so. That was the time Wendy left with a member of my staff. Al St. John. You've met him, Ms. Goosens."

"Of course," she said. It was impossible to tell if she remembered Al at all. Nuns are supposed to be serene, and lawyers practice not looking surprised, so it was hard to read anything from Livia Goosens's face.

"Still," she said, "there is nothing to tell us that *you* might not have switched the bottles, Mr. Cobb. You had, by your own admission, some seven hours of opportunity, during part of which, at least, I assume Miss Ichimi was asleep."

I looked at her. For a long time. Finally I said, "Am I under arrest?"

She was spared the necessity of backing down, or even worse, having to to put me under arrest, by the arrival of Detective Gumple. "News from the lab, Lieutenant."

I was impressed. They were right on top of this one.

Gumple is the type who won't go on without encouragement. Lieutenant Martin humored him. "Well, what the hell *is* the news from the lab, goddammit?"

"It was this DMSO stuff, all right." He reached into his pocket and brought out a battered notebook. "It was mixed with some kind of cyanide compound, like they use in developing film. They're not sure what, yet."

"Great," the lieutenant snarled.

"Yeah," Rivetz said, "try tracing it. Especially if they don't nail down which one."

"The lab also doesn't know what the dosage was, because . . ." he peered closely at his notes, "because 'the interdermal properties of dimethylsulfoxide have not been sufficiently well determined to enable us to say how much of a dissolved substance will penetrate the subcutaneous fat and enter the bloodstream.' " Gumple looked up at us with a vague smile of accomplishment.

"She rubbed it on her *ankle* for Christ's sake," I said. "How much subcutaneous fat is there to worry about there?"

The Frying Nun brought the meeting back under control. "Whatever the dosage, it was fatal, and that is our only concern at present. Mr. Cobb. When and how was that bottle switched?"

I had had about enough of this woman. I hadn't known Bea Dunney long or well, but I liked her as much as you can like anyone on that kind of acquaintance. Less than three hours ago Bea Dunney had died horribly before my eyes, and ADA Goosens was using it as a chance to twit me. To hell with her.

"Objection, counselor," I said.

That amused her. "On what grounds?"

"Calls for a conclusion on the part of the witness. Not the best evidence."

Lieutenant Martin started to laugh. "Sustained, Matty. Sustained. He's got you Ms. Goosens. You want to know what happened to that bag, you've got to talk to Wendy Ichimi or Cobb's man, St. John. They were with it all day."

It must be hard to speak without moving a single muscle, not even your lips, but the Frying Nun managed it somehow. "Oh, I'll speak to them. Both of them. Have Miss Ichimi brought up here."

Helena Speir came along; ADA Goosens said it was okay, she had questions for her, too. The stepmother kept trying to take Wendy's hand, and Wendy kept shaking loose.

Wendy did not look well. She was back in street clothes, but somehow she didn't seem to fill them; she looked like a bundle of rags wrapped around a stick. Her face was strange, too. There were marks of recent tears, and her eyes were large and liquid, but aside from that, there was no sign of emotion. Damn near no sign of life.

"Miss Ichimi," the Frying Nun said politely enough, "my name is Livia Goosens. I am the assistant district attorney assigned to this case—"

"He meant to kill me, didn't he?" Wendy said. She was looking at me.

"What makes you say that, Miss Ichimi?"

There was life in Wendy's face now. Ms. Goosen caught an accumulated store of fear, frustration, and anger. *"Don't be stupid!"* Wendy hissed. "And don't treat me as if you think I'm stupid!" She started to laugh, not her usual laugh. Not a pretty sound. "Why, no less an authority than the famous psychiatrist Paul Dinkover said I was unusually gifted. I got a great gift today, didn't I?"

Helena Speir wanted to get Wendy out of there, a move that struck me as a healthy idea, but Wendy would have none of it.

"I'm all *right,*" she insisted. "I just want to know. Come on, Matt. No lies," she said. "We're friends, right?"

"Right," I said.

"It was *me* he was trying to kill. Wasn't it?"

No official tried to prevent me from answering her. They wouldn't have succeeded if they'd tried. "It looks that way, Wendy."

Wendy nodded. "I thought so. It was my DMSO. Bea never used it, never needed to. She used to joke about her strong joints, how she never even got a charley horse. How she was going to skate forever. It couldn't have been meant for her. No one could have known she was even going to use it."

She swallowed. "Somebody wanted me to use it. Poison DMSO. It was only a matter of time before I would have. If Bea hadn't fallen on the ice today, I'd be the one who was dead." She looked at me again. "Wouldn't I?"

What do you say to someone in a situation like that? The silence hung over the office like a mist until Detective First Grade Horace A. Rivetz, who, prior to this, I had never seen display an ounce of sentiment, said exactly the right thing.

"Relax, kid," he told Wendy, "it wasn't your turn today. That's all there is to it. Don't drive yourself nuts over it."

Lieutenant Martin stared at Rivetz as if he'd grown bat wings; I sneaked a look at him myself. I couldn't stare because Wendy had another question.

"Does anybody know why?"

"Not yet," I said.

Wendy nodded, as if to say it was silly to have expected anything else. Then, all hostility gone, she turned to Livia Goosens and said, "What do you want to know?"

She wanted to know who had the opportunity to get into her bag. Wendy tried to oblige. First there was the group at Brother's office: Brother, Danov, Mrs. Speir (who was more than a little upset to hear her name mentioned in this context; Ms. Goosens assured her it was just routine); Carla Nelson Dinkover, and Wendy herself.

"I hope nobody thinks I wanted to kill Bea," she said. "We were friends."

"How could you have made her need to use the DMSO?" I said, and the assistant district attorney shot me a look that could have burned the bark off an oak. I subsided, but I was glad I'd reassured Wendy.

The second group of people boiled down to the World at Large. Wendy had left her bag on the sidewalk while she'd signed autographs outside the Garden. It had been near her, but she hadn't seen anybody mess with it, just as she hadn't seen anybody go near her bag in her agent's office. Which was not to say she would necessarily have noticed if anyone had. Sorry.

Lieutenant Martin decided it was time to assert himself, and addressed the same questions to Wendy's stepmother, who got indignant again.

"Someone has tried to kill my daughter! And instead of finding the real killer you treat *us* like criminals." I'm not kidding, she really said that. She had more, too, but I tuned out. The cops were having some trouble paying attention, too.

Once she got it out of her system, she was fairly cooperative. She wasn't any help, but she was cooperative. She hadn't seen anything either.

The Frying Nun was just about to excuse them when Gumple opened the door and ushered in Max Brother. Below the cheekbones, the agent was as smooth and well dressed as always. Above them, he was a mess. His eyes kept jumping around, as though they were trying to escape the purple pouches he now kept them in. His forehead was grooved from the eyebrows halfway to the hairline.

Brother's voice was fine, but the things he said were off. For instance, when he was brought in, the first words out of his mouth were, "So this is the experimental control room. Amazing how compact it all is." I got the impression that Brother had decided to say that the first time he saw the room, and the mess this afternoon had knocked him onto automatic pilot.

"I understand you and the victim have been intimate in recent months." Trust the Frying Nun to bring him back to the point. Furthermore, it showed she wasn't letting any grass grow under her—she'd turned up (or more likely some cop had) that little tidbit in no time at all. Probably got it from one of the girls in the show.

As it turned out, bringing him back to the point had probably been a tactical error. The question hit him like a bucket of cold water. He shivered, blinked, and straightened out into the Max Brother I'd known before.

"Yes," he said. "Yes, we were. Bea was a wonderful girl and a fine talent. Not a talent like Wendy, of course, but Bea had a special quality that was quite unique."

I wanted to tell him nothing can be quite unique. "Unique" means one of a kind; something is either unique or it isn't, and that's that. I didn't say anything, though, despite this phrase's unique (see?) ability to make my teeth grind together. Somehow, I thought it just wouldn't be appreciated.

Actually, my pique at Brother's diction was just a symptom of a general antsiness I'd been feeling for quite a while. Seeing people die and bandying words with clever lawyers are two of my least favorite ways to spend an afternoon two days before Christmas.

Brother was taking a few seconds to speak to Wendy and Helena Speir; it was terrible, and they had all lost a friend. He didn't get much of a response.

Helena Speir asked if she and Wendy could leave; Livia Goosens gave them permission and didn't even write them out a pass. She offered Wendy police protection; Wendy turned it down.

Both Max Brother and her stepmother were aghast. I wasn't too pleased about it myself, but Wendy was adamant. Wouldn't explain, either. The only thing she would say was that she wanted to talk to me outside.

I was ready to go, and the Frying Nun was ready to get rid of me. I was under orders not to leave the building without permission, not that I would have, anyway. I might not have wanted to stick around and hear Max Brother's every word, but I intended to find out what he had said.

Outside in the hallway, Wendy put her hand on my chest and pushed me about twenty yards down the curving corridor, away from her stepmother.

"I talked with the road manager of the show," Wendy said softly. I could see Helena Speir looking at a picture of Walt Frazier on the wall, pretending she wasn't trying to rabbit-ear the conversation. "Before I was sent for. I've decided something—there's going to be a show tonight, but I'm not going to be in it."

"Sounds like a good idea to me," I told her. "But why don't you let the cops assign someone to you? It doesn't have to be obtru—"

"No!" she said in a voice loud enough to spin the head of the older woman in our direction.

"You're being overheard," I told Wendy.

"No," she said again, quietly but just as intensely. "I hate this. I'm isolated enough already. I don't need police around reinforcing it."

"Your logic," I told her, "eludes me. If you don't have a guard, you'll be isolated in your room across the street with your stepmother."

"No, I won't," she said. It occurred to me that the old canard about Orientals being inscrutable was just so much bullshit. Wendy's face was a picture window to what was in her brain. What was in her brain that moment was determination, or to be less diplomatic about it, pigheadedness.

"Wendy, I hate to be a spoilsport, but you put your finger on it yourself in there. *Somebody tried to kill you today.*"

She jumped as if a cat had scratched her.

"I'm sorry, but it's a fact that has to be faced. When something like that happens, it doesn't go away if you ignore it. You can *hope* he'll have some kind of miraculous reformation, or get hit by a truck, before he tries again, but it's just silly to take it for granted."

"No police. I want to stay with you again."

Helena Speir strode to us, her sensible shoes slapping on the hard floor. Rabbit ears was right—she'd heard every word of it.

"You will *not* stay with the man," she declared.

"Don't tell me what to do, Helena," her stepdaughter said.

"You don't know him. You met him only a week ago. How can you possibly trust him more than the police?"

"Knowing someone a long time doesn't mean you can trust him," Wendy said. "How long did my father know Dinkover? How long did you know him? You even went to bed with him—"

Helena Speir was a big, strong woman, and when she lashed out and smacked Wendy, the sound of the blow echoed around that whole circular corridor. Wendy bent sideways to forty-five degrees, then snapped back vertical.

I figured I was about to have to step between two angry women, but it didn't turn out that way. Wendy and her stepmother stood in identical attitudes. Each of them stood staring, with a hand to her face; Wendy in pain, Helena Speir shocked by what she had done.

Then it was my turn to be shocked. The stepmother turned a face red with anger on me. "This is your fault!" she hissed.

I have faced some bum raps in my life, but this one took the trophy. For one thing, I also thought it was imprudent on Wendy's part to be putting her life in my hands on such a short acquaintance and one night's intimacy.

I was going to say so, but I couldn't get a word in edgewise. I had seduced her little girl. (Wendy said, in a deadly voice, that she was not a little girl.) I was a fortune hunter attempting to cut myself in for a piece of Wendy's money and fame; the money and fame she (Helena Speir) had worked and sacrificed so long to see that she attained. And more, even less justified.

Finally, Wendy said, "That does it," and hauled me off. It was just as well. I have a temper that needs to be kept under tight control, and it was beginning to slip. I was maybe three seconds from saying something I was going to regret.

As we walked back to the office/control room to rejoin the police, Wendy's stepmother yelled after me that I hadn't heard the last of this. I was sure I hadn't.

When she finally gave up and left, I took Wendy aside and asked her how her face felt.

"It stings. Not as bad as she used to be."

"She used to beat you?" I could feel my temper sliding away again.

"Oh, she didn't *beat* me," Wendy began. Then she made a face that had more anger and pain in it than the one she wore when the blow landed. "Oh, screw her. Yes, she did beat me. Or at least she hit me. She hasn't done it for years. She went to a shrink after the divorce from that bastard Speir, and she never did it any more."

"Until now," I said.

Wendy took my hand. "Matt, look, I don't want to give you the wrong idea. She never used a wire coat hanger on me or anything. It was just like she did this time, a smack across the face or two."

"Oh," I said. "A mere bagatelle, right? When did she do it?"

"When I didn't want to practice. She used to say I should be happy I was small and graceful and pretty, and not big and clumsy the way she was. That it was a sin not to develop my gifts; that it was an insult to her, but I was wasting things she'd kill for."

"Come on, I'll get them to get a cop to take you home."

"I'm staying with *you*," she insisted.

"Yes, you are staying with me. But only because I think you're twit enough to insist on no cops even if I say no."

"I want to be with you. I trust you."

"Yeah," I said. "You keep saying you're not a child, but you sure keep acting like one." Wendy opened her mouth. "Quiet," I said. I reached into my pocket and took out my keys. "I can't leave until the ADA lets me go. We'll get a cop to see you to my place—I'm better than nothing, I guess."

"A little," she conceded.

"Okay, then. My apartment—"

"I thought you said it wasn't your apartment."

"A technicality. My apartment, my rules. Got that?"

"Yes." She looked as if she wanted to say something else, but the look on my face convinced her not to.

"Good. Now. The cop will take you home. I will have called the doorman to let him know you're coming. The cop will accompany you to the apartment and check the place out. You will lock the door, and bolt it, and you will let no one in but me. Then you will play with Spot. I'll walk him tonight. His dog food is under the sink. Should I repeat any of that?"

She said it wasn't necessary. I raised my hand to knock on the door, but before I could, Wendy said, "Matt?"

"What is it?"

"You're really taking this seriously, aren't you?"

"Can't afford not to."

"Matt, I'm scared." Her eyes seconded the statement.

"We'll get him. Or her. Just be careful."

"I will. I'm sorry to be such a pill."

I couldn't deny she was being a pill, so I just smiled at her and went inside and got her sent home.

*"Now here he is, America's Top Trader,
TV's Big Dealer . . ."*
—Jay Stewart, *Let's Make a Deal*
(ABC)

CHAPTER THIRTEEN

Two hours later, I left the Garden and stepped into the cold air. The sky was pitch dark and overcast, but of course it never gets very dark in New York, unless Con Edison screws up. Right now, happy crowds were converging on the arena to line up for tonight's Ice-Travaganza. I wondered how many would want their money back after they found out Wendy wouldn't be appearing tonight. I decided probably not many. The Christmas spirit and all that—give the understudy a chance.

The Christmas spirit was all around me that night. People were smiling, noticing each other. Not everybody, of course; there is a class of New Yorker who becomes mute if he doesn't call somebody an asshole every twenty seconds. But there were enough happy people walking decorated streets, carrying packages, under the black sky and the orangey sodium vapor lamps. Enough to make a difference.

I was not one of them, and it bothered me. I think that was the thing that I disliked most about this case—it was screwing up my Christmas. Christmas is the time I try to set aside to let the real me come out. What I like to think is the real me, the undisillusioned, unsophisticated kid who used to feel like smiling all year round. At least that's the way I look to myself through the lens of Christmastime nostalgia.

But that kid was nowhere in sight, this year. Here it was, December

23 (and pushing 7 P.M. at that), and I hadn't had a glimpse of him. I was hoping he'd show up, but I wasn't optimistic. Somehow, I don't think that kid would get much of a kick out of dead people and murder suspects. He might enjoy taking care of a damsel in distress, as long as the shit didn't get too thick. Maybe I'd find him back at the apartment with Wendy, but I doubted it.

I might as well have stayed with Wendy all along, as far as progress in the case was concerned. Max Brother had gotten back one hundred percent of his aplomb and had contributed nothing new except that he had made the movie deal for Bea before they ever became intimate. He said. I'd just as soon flip a coin for the truth of that one. A woman can be grateful for something an agent or a producer's done, but in show biz, it's not unheard of for gratitude to go through a sort of time warp, and arrive before the deed that's going to cause it.

Brother, as usual, had pressing business matters to attend to, especially in the wake of this "terrible, terrible, thing," and he was going to have to fight off his own "great personal sadness" and put things together again. The Frying Nun excused him, but before I left, I thought I caught him giving me (of all people) the old hairy eyeball. He was gone before I could get any clue why.

Ivan Danov was next, exploding all over the place, with waterworks to go with the usual pyrotechnics.

"It is *terrible!*" he sobbed. That word was getting a real workout. "*Doubly* terrible!"

The Frying Nun seemed intimidated, or maybe only repelled by all this unbridled emotion. Whatever the reason, she lay back and let Lieutenant Martin handle the questioning.

"How's that, Mr. Danov?"

Danov didn't insist on his constitutional rights before answering.

"Well, it is a horror that poor Beatrice is dead. She was a fine skater; it was a crime her training had to end. She would have been a creditable international skater—certainly one of the ten or twenty best in the world."

"Gold medal material?"

"Bah! She was a beautiful girl; she had talent. But a gold medal? Never, as long as Wendy was alive."

There are sentences that get bigger after they're uttered. This one expanded into a dead silence big enough to fill the whole Garden.

Danov began to sob again. "But that is the other thing! I have heard this . . . this *vandal* wanted to kill Wendy! My Wendy, whom I have molded into the finest skater alive!"

He stood up. *"It must not happen!"* he declaimed. He had one hand across his chest and the other in the air. The pose made him look like a statue.

"Cobb!" he yelled, as though he had just invented a name for me. "They tell me *you* have become responsible for Wendy's safety!"

"Reluctantly," I admitted. I was glad I wasn't counting on secrecy for Wendy's protection. Gossip travels fast, but this was ridiculous. I decided Helena Speir was stopping people on the street and telling them that I had abducted her child.

Danov walked up to me, held his angular face about five inches from mine, and said, "If any harm comes to her, if she suffers so much as a bruise, you will answer to *Danov!*"

After a scene like that, mere questioning was an anticlimax, especially since Danov swore up and down that no one had tampered with Wendy's bag in his presence. Was he a fool? Would he not have noticed?

It went on like that. After a while, the cops got tired and let him go. He repeated his warning to me before he left.

When the door closed behind him, Livia Goosens said, "You'll answer to much more than Danov if anything happens to the girl, Cobb."

"Up yours," I said suavely. "What the hell was I supposed to do?"

"Convince her she needs professional protection," the ADA said.

"I'm working on it, for Christ's sake."

"I suggest you continue to do so, Mr. Cobb. Her safety is in your hands."

Didn't I know it. The ADA smiled a superior smile and said she was going back to her office to await the arrival of other witnesses, namely Carla Dinkover and Al St. John. I was more or less ordered to find St. John, which I promised to do. I'd call the Network and have him beeped (see how *he* liked it), but not until I was home.

Lieutenant Martin looked at me and shook his head. "I don't know,

Matty," he said. "Most guys are content just to bring home puppy dogs."

Rivetz laughed. I told them I already had a puppy dog, and left.

An afternoon that begins with my watching someone die and ends with my trading feeble quips with the police is not one that's likely to inspire me with the Christmas spirit.

It is, in fact, the kind of afternoon that makes me downright nasty; that's why I was taking a stroll before heading uptown. Wendy was going to be a big enough pain to deal with when I was in full control of myself.

A hand grabbed my shoulder. It wasn't a blow, or even the kind of arm a cop puts on you when he wants your attention. It was something more than a tap, but that's all.

I didn't care. Visions of Harris Brophy danced in my head. Granted this was Thirty-fourth Street in the early evening and not West Tenth late at night, I wasn't about to stand still for a going over with a wrench, if that's what the person had in mind.

I ducked and spun to my left, knocking the arm away with my left forearm. At the same time, I launched a punch with my right fist, which I stopped about an eighth of an inch from the throat of Max Brother.

"Oh, for Christ's sake," I said, dropping my hands. "What the hell do *you* want?"

Brother's face was wild. "Cobb, what are you nuts? That punch landed, I would have been *dead.*"

"Maybe," I said. "I don't like to fight, so I try to get them over in a hurry. Besides, I'm jumpy. There's a killer or two running around. Did you follow me?"

Brother nodded. "I waited around in the bookstore near the Garden. I almost didn't spot you. I followed you because I didn't want the police to see us talking."

"Oh? Why not?"

"I have something to tell you. In confidence."

"Well, that's great. Only how do you know the police don't have a tail on you?"

He turned white. In the unnatural light of the street lamp, he looked like a corpse. "Why . . . why should they do that?"

"Use your brain. You are present at the scene of one sensational murder; then your girlfriend gets killed in another. And you had the opportunity to switch the jars."

"But I didn't do it," he insisted.

"The cops like to be convinced."

It's amazing how, in times of stress, people fall back on doing whatever it is they do for a living. Right now, Brother was trying to negotiate with me.

"But Cobb," he said. Mr. Consensus. "I don't mean to get personal, but just for the sake of argument, what you've said about me could apply to you, too, with just a few changes. You were on the scene of Dinkover's murder. You found the body, in fact. And *your* girlfriend—or at least the girl you spent the night with . . ."

I wondered if there was anybody in the United States who didn't know that yet.

". . . was the *target* of the second murder. You can't deny poor Bea was killed by mistake."

The epithet had the sound of permanence to it. It encapsulated her and dismissed her in one breath. From now on, Max Brother would never speak of her except with the words "Poor Bea."

"Besides," he went on, "you had more opportunity to switch those bottles than anybody."

"Absolutely right," I said. "How do you know the cops don't have a tail on me?"

Brother started looking around him as if his head were mounted on a balance wheel. "Do you think they have?"

"No," I said, and Brother let out about a bushel of air. "When it looked as if I was going to deck you, your tail or mine would probably have intervened. But what's the big secret?"

"I have to be absolutely sure we're not overheard."

"Why? Why come to me?"

"You seem to be an honest man." To my surprise, Brother smiled. It wasn't his business smile, either. "In my line of work, you don't meet too many. Besides, you seem to have pull with the cops." He smiled again. "Listen to me. Slipping back to the city and the streets. I've trained myself to say things like 'influence with the police' instead."

I was fully aware that this might be a ploy. The "come on, no secrets, we're all friends here" approach is ancient. Still, he did it well, and I was a lot more disposed to hear what he had to say. Besides, I was getting pretty curious.

"Cobb, I mean this. I've been sitting on something hot, and I'm getting scorched. I'm going to put my life in your hands."

"That's swell," I said, "but I make you no promises. If I hush up something that hot, my life is in *your* hands."

Brother nodded. "Sure, I can appreciate that. But you will help me if you can?"

"No promises."

"All right, all right. Where can we go to talk?"

"Let's go Christmas shopping."

It wasn't as crazy as it sounds. I took him to Herald Square, where Sixth Avenue (Avenue of the Americas, for you out-of-towners) and Broadway cross at Thirty-fourth Street. It's the world's busiest intersection, and at Christmas, it's even busier. We went inside Macy's, which is the World's Largest Store under one roof, a whole block's worth of an eight-story building, every inch of it crammed with shoppers.

A big department store is a great place to find out if you've got a tail. If you're in a big hurry, you can do something dramatic, like fight your way up the down escalator. Otherwise, you can work a few tricks with the elevators. In general, though, because of the masses of bodies, and the difficulty of getting anywhere, it's impossible for someone to follow you without your knowledge if you just know what to look for.

There didn't seem to be anybody following us, which made the whole trip unnecessary. I didn't mind, though—I still had some Christmas shopping to do.

In the book department, I got a book about famous con men for Harris. It's boring to be in a hospital, especially after you start getting well. There was a book about eagles; I picked it up and looked at it, but it wasn't much help, unless Dinkover had been trying to tell us he had been killed by a real eagle, which I doubted.

As long as I was at it, I took a look at one of those huge one-volume encyclopedias for the article about flags. I learned that the study of flags is called vexillology; that the usual proportions for a flag are ten by nineteen; and that the "stars and stripes" are more properly called "mullets and barrulets." I didn't learn anything about the case.

I also hadn't learned, yet, what Brother had on his mind. As we went to the checkout, I said, "You wanted to talk to me, but I'm not hearing anything."

"There are all these people around," he protested.

"Speak quietly, and don't mention any names. Nobody will pay the slightest attention. Christmas shopping is a pretty absorbing experience."

Brother didn't like it, but he didn't have much choice, aside from forgetting the whole thing. I didn't think he'd do that. He swallowed a couple of times, looked around, then began.

"I let him in," he said.

"*What?!*" I practically screamed it. Five thousand harried Christmas shoppers got unabsorbed enough to gawk at me. So much for telling Brother to be cool.

I had to try to redeem myself. "Why, that's *wonderful,* Max," I gushed. "You'll have to tell me all about it." Heads looked away; we were just a couple of businessmen sharing some good news. Much more quietly, I said, "Tell me all about it, Max."

"I knew we shouldn't have done it here." He was nervous again.

"Did you kill him?"

"God almighty, Cobb. No. I got a phone call from Di—"

"No names."

"From the old man that afternoon. He told me to fix one of the exit doors so he could get in and talk to Wendy. He told me to push a button on the door that would keep it from latching."

It was interesting Dinkover should have known the construction of the doors at the Blades Club well enough to give that kind of instruction.

But that wasn't the most interesting part. "The old man called you and told you to do this, huh?"

"Yes."

"Why the hell did you do it?"

Brother swallowed again, then brushed at a head of hair that needed no brushing. "That's the hard part."

I wanted to laugh. "The hard part is coming up? Listen, do you know what would happen to you if you told Lieutenant Martin what you've told me so far?"

"I'd be arrested for murder," he said. It was about halfway to a question, as though Brother cherished a small foolish hope he might be wrong.

"At least," I told him. "Why did you let him in? Did you know what was going to happen?"

Brother was irritated. "Cobb, do you think I would be telling you this if I was involved in Din—I mean in what happened to the old man? To anybody?" By anybody, he meant Poor Bea. "I'd be running for my life; turning state's evidence; trying to tough it out.

"I'm scared, Cobb. I've got to figure out some way to get this case solved without ruining my life."

"Good. You keep figuring. Meanwhile, you are going to answer my question right now, or I am bringing you to the nearest cop. Now. For the third and last time, why did you let him in?"

"He blackmailed me into it."

"Over what?"

"Coke."

"I'm warning you, Brother."

"I'm telling you the truth!"

"How the hell can he be blackmailing you over cocaine? It was on the cover of *People* magazine, for Christ's sake. Besides, I thought you kicked it."

"I did." The agent sounded bitter.

"Well? Sounds like something you'd want spread around. Not much blackmail potential there."

"Look, Cobb, you don't understand."

"No argument on that." It was my turn to pay for the book. I paid cash, and the girl behind the counter seemed grateful enough to faint.

"This is nice," she said. "All day, punching buttons, and I'm getting a fat wrist from the embossing machine. Merry Christmas."

I smiled at her and took my package. The smile was to make up for the dirty look Max Brother gave her. He had no patience for pleasantries now that he'd started to talk.

"Can we get out of here now?" he demanded.

"One more stop," I said, and we headed for the escalator. "Keep talking."

"All right, it was on the cover of a magazine. Do you remember what it was all about?"

"Sure," I said. "You and your ex-wife are having a custody fight over your daughter." Brother's ex-wife was also an agent; there had been jokes about how it was the first time in the history of show business that two agents had agreed in advance to be screwed by each other. When they'd decided to split up, that joke took on a whole new meaning. Both husband and wife were used to looking for an edge, used to getting it. It looked like the winner would be decided on the basis of Who Gets The Kid, and the fight was still going on. A California judge had awarded custody to Mrs. Brother, but Max had vowed never to give up.

"Yeah, my daughter. I have to get her back, Cobb; that bitch I was married to is no good for her. I have to."

I had no idea of the Brothers' relative merits as parents; it just seemed to me that the main reason Brother wanted custody was to prove he was tougher than his wife was.

"The only thing is," Brother continued, "these goddam lawyers cost a fortune; I was overextended, badly. I needed cash in a hurry, so I did something stupid."

"Meddle with a client's money?" I was ragging him. I knew what he was leading up to.

"Of course not. What do you think I am, a crook?" He looked almost hurt. "I was just in a bind; my clients are my life. I sell them out, I'm a dead man."

It was easy to see Brother was serious. His life was built around being a Big Shot, being the man rich and famous people came to for advice. He'd come too far to want to blow it.

It was making it difficult to say what he wanted to say. The hell of it was, I already knew.

Brother worked on it. For the first time since the book department, he looked to see who was in earshot. He lowered his voice even further. "I sold some cocaine," he said.

I nodded. "In April," I told him. I told him the names of the director and actress he sold it to, as well.

"You son of a bitch!" he hissed. "You've been stringing me along the whole time."

"Not the whole time," I argued. "Just a few minutes. I wanted to see if you'd come across with some cock and bull story, or maybe confess to something I *didn't* know about."

"But this was secret. *Tomb* secret. How did you find out?" Sweat was beginning to break out on his forehead. If I knew, and the blackmailer knew, how secret could it all be?

"I found out because Shorty Stack filed a report on you when the Network was thinking about making the deal for Wendy's special."

"Oh, God," Brother said. "I should have known."

Shorty Stack was assistant vice-president, Special Projects, West Coast. He functioned with a large degree in autonomy, and he caused a certain amount of fear. Shorty had begun as a legman for Louella Parsons, until a certain studio decided he was too dangerous to be allowed to run loose. It was said that Shorty Stack must be under every bed in Hollywood. They hired him to find out things before they got into gossip columns and to stop them before they did. He was the most feared man in Hollywood, even though few people had seen him or even knew what he looked like. He was supposed to be working for me, but I'd never laid eyes on him, either.

Shorty went to work for the Network when the studio he'd worked for reduced its operations drastically in the late sixties. Times were more tolerant, so Shorty didn't have the impact he used to, but his name was still enough to bring a reaction of awe, fear, or hatred, depending on the state of the hearer's conscience. The only reason he didn't have my job was that he refused to leave California under any circumstances.

"Who have you told about this?" Brother demanded. He grabbed my sleeve and said it again.

"Relax, for crying out loud. I haven't told anybody outside my own staff. No reason to."

"You could have told me that you knew, at least."

"Look, I know you're upset, but try to use your head. There was no reason to mention it. For one thing, if the Network refused to do business with anybody who'd ever taken part in a drug deal, there'd be nothing on the air but test patterns. For another thing, even if we wanted to, we didn't have any evidence. Shorty hears things, that's all.

He has people he believes. There was nothing that would be useful in a court."

"Screw that. Who knows what's going to influence a judge? That guy is nuts. Look, it's a matter of image, all right? I was a big coke head; I stopped using it; now I'm a hero. If it comes out that after I stopped using it, I turn around and score a big deal on it, what am I? A cynical sleaze."

It was hard to resist looking at him and saying, "Well?" But I managed.

"You saw what happened to De Lorean, didn't you? That could have been me. It still could."

"Yes, it could."

"And this goddam blackmailer. How did he find out?"

"That's not important; if Shorty found out, anybody could. From here, it looks like the blackmailer was the killer." I didn't tell him that this also made it look as if the killer had to be one of the party at the Blades Club last night. "You want the killer caught."

"I want my kid."

I made a purchase, paid for it, and led Brother out of the store onto Sixth Avenue. He took a deep breath of the cold air, than another one. He had the look of a man who's just clawed his way out of a plastic bag.

"You want the murderer caught," I said again.

"Of course I do. Don't you think I'm human at all? Poor Bea was a great kid. But I can't bring her back."

My turn to take a deep breath. I did it so I wouldn't break his jaw. "Did it ever occur to you," I said quietly, "that if you had been straight with the police, Bea might not have gone anywhere?"

"I want my daughter, Cobb. I can't let this get out."

"I made no promises. The cops have to know. But I think I know how to minimize the grief for you."

Christmas had just come for Max Brother. You could see it in his face. "There's no limit to what I would owe you if you could help me, Cobb. None."

"Just tell me about the phone call."

"Reach out and touch someone."
—Bell Telephone commercial

CHAPTER FOURTEEN

I handed Wendy a package and said, "Here, Merry Christmas."

She said what people always say in that situation: "For *me?*"

"Of course for you. Spot gets his present Christmas morning; my mother makes him some special turkey giblet dog food."

"That's sweet," Wendy said. "Matt, where have you been? I was beginning to worry about you."

"I've been talking with your manager, not about business."

"Oh. About the case?" I nodded. "You have to tell me about this. Right?"

"I don't know about have to. I think I will; you deserve to know about it. Did I get any calls?"

"Your mother called. Lieutenant Martin, too. He sounded angry." I told her it figured. She held up the package. "Should I open this now or wait?"

It wasn't unprecedented for my mother to call me and have a woman answer the phone, but it always led to some interesting reactions. I could hardly wait. "Go ahead and open it," I said. "What did my mother want?"

"She left the message on the tape," Wendy said. "Something about church. A lot of stuff. I didn't think it would be a good idea to answer the phone."

"That was smart," I said.

"You don't have to act so surprised."

I smiled at her. "Don't I? After you spurned police protection?"

"I'm sorry, Matt. Dammit, I—I don't know what I'm doing any more. Maybe it was dumb—it just felt better this way. I'm safe now, right?"

"I think so."

Wendy looked wretched. "Matt, I swear to God, I never hurt anybody in my life. It's not fair that somebody wants to kill me. And Bea. Bea was the closest thing to a friend I had. She never hurt anybody either."

I joined her on the couch and put my arm around her. She sat looking at her hands.

It was Spot who saved the day. Spot has such a fascination with bags and boxes, I sometimes think he must be part cat. Somehow, in his sniffing around, he'd managed to get his head caught in the bag Wendy's present had been in. Now he was running around, shaking his head violently, trying to get it off. Wendy laughed at him in spite of herself.

"The Unknown Dog," I said, and Wendy laughed harder. I went to check out my phone messages while Wendy finished opening her gift.

My mother was getting pretty insistent about my showing up in church dressed and shaved and with my ears open ten o'clock Christmas morning to hear my sister solo with the choir. It would also be nice, she said, if I received communion, but that was a bargaining ploy.

It was a pleasure to be able to call her up and tell her that I would be there at the appointed time. The way things looked now, it would be a lot easier to catch the real thing than go to a rehearsal the day before, the way I'd originally planned.

Everything was sweetness and light in the family when I hung up and returned to Wendy. My houseguest was holding a light blue garment against her body. She looked pleased, but puzzled.

"I guess it will fit," she said, "and I do need a nightgown, I guess, if I'm going to be staying here, but why *flannel?*"

"I *like* flannel," I told her. "I think it's much sexier than the sheer stuff."

"You're weird."

"Also, it's December. Cold sometimes, even in a luxury apartment."

"Weird and practical," Wendy said. "What a combination. But thanks, Matt." She gave me a kiss. "I don't have anything for you."

"Not necessary. Look, I have to call Lieutenant Martin, then I'll tell you about Brother."

I never got a chance to. The switchboard man at Headquarters was altogether too eager to patch me through to the lieutenant, and the lieutenant yelled so loud, it practically made the phone superfluous.

"At last!" he said. "I was afraid everybody connected with this goddam case had disappeared."

"I told you I'd call you as soon as I got home."

"Yeah, you told me. You also told me you'd put me in touch with your man, St. John. The bimbo at the Network switchboard won't even beep him for me."

"Of course not," I said. "It's his day off. Only I can reach him."

"Well?" Before I could answer (not that I could say much—it *had* slipped my mind), the lieutenant went on. "Not only that, but I couldn't reach *you.* We haven't been able to get in touch with Mrs. Dinkover—I'll tell you more about that in a second—and that goddam agent has vanished."

"Ah," I said.

"Ah?" Lieutenant Martin echoed. "*Ah?* Matty, why do you want to make an old man exasperated? Do you know something about where Brother is?"

"I know everything about where Brother is. I took him there."

"This better be good," the lieutenant warned.

"You may not like this," I said.

"I already don't like it. What did you do? Put him on a plane to the Mato Grosso?"

"I brought him to the Drug Enforcement Agency. He's going to talk to them about cocaine." I told him Max Brother's story, concluding with how I decided the only way to keep Brother from getting destroyed by the publicity that would follow the revelation that he had been the one who let Dinkover into the Blades Club would be to get a government agency to protect him. Ralph Goodrum at the DEA had said he would be delighted to hear anything Brother cared to tell him about coke traffic, especially anything about who the big suppliers to the Hollywood scene might be. When I left, they were even making noises to use Brother to set up a sting operation, if they liked what they heard.

Lieutenant Martin didn't like what he heard. "Matty," he said. He sounded too shocked even to yell at me. "I can't believe you did this. This is the first thing that resembles a break in the case. Brother let him in—is this straight? Brother really told you he let him in?"

"With his own lips."

"Then how in hell could you give the son of a bitch to the goddam Feds?! This could bust the case wide open!"

"Not unless Brother is the killer."

"Not unless Brother is the killer! Jesus H. Moses, Matty, if the Frying Nun wasn't such a tight ass, he could probably be indicted on that alone!"

"Ralph Goodrum promised me Brother would be there all night and available any time you wanted to talk to him."

"Who cares what he promised *you?* I haven't trusted a federal official since 1944."

"What happened in 1944?"

"I was drafted."

"Good point. Why don't you call Goodrum right away and let him make you a promise, too?"

"I will, as soon as we hang up here. Now listen, Matty. I'm going to let this go for now, but we're gonna have a long talk, real soon. Now, here's what I want you to do. You get on the phone to the Network, and you tell that uppity wench on the switchboard to beep your man, St. John, and you and him both meet me at this address." He gave me the number of a building on Fifth Avenue.

"Where's that?" I asked.

"Dinkover's apartment."

"Oh," I said. I remembered Wendy had thought that Dinkover was a neighbor of mine. Actually, it turned out he had lived on the park, but on the other side of it. Almost directly across as it turned out.

"Your wish is my command, of course . . ."

"Bull*shit,*" the lieutenant said, giving it the standard New York City street pronunciation.

". . . But why are we going there?"

"You're going there because I want to talk to St. John and kick your treacherous behind, and I have to do it in person, and that's where I'm going to be. I'm going to be there because Goosens has managed to convince herself that the widow Dinkover has taken a run-out powder."

"Careful, Mr. M., you're dating yourself." He made a noise. "Do you know why she thinks so?"

"Nobody answers the phone in the Dinkover apartment. Nobody answers the door. The doorman says nobody's gone in or out of the building, at least past him. So if anybody came or went, they sneaked it. The ADA doesn't like it."

"I wouldn't think you'd be too crazy about it yourself. Couldn't your men have gotten the super to let them in?"

"It's legal enough, but between the press being on us because everybody involved is so famous, and being picked at by the Frying Nun, we're walking on eggs around here. We put in for a warrant to go inside, should come through any second—we'll be super legal this way. Covering our ass. Hell of a way to do police work. You just be there, you hear?"

"I'll be there."

"Your pal, too."

"Right."

"I heard a lot of that." Wendy was standing right behind me.

"Sneak up on me like that again, and I'm going to put a bell around your neck."

"I wanted to know what was keeping you."

"All right, it doesn't matter. I said I'd tell you, anyway. You just startled me for a second."

"Max was dealing in drugs?"

"Coke," I said.

"That's a drug," she said, and I certainly couldn't argue with her. "I think I *will* fire him. I don't need that kind of thing anywhere near my career. Or my life."

"Yeah," I said. "Basically, I agree with you."

"You don't sound like it."

"Not because I'm not against coke. In the last couple of years, I've seen fortunes, careers, and lives sucked up nostrils."

"What's the problem, then?"

"I sort of made an implied promise to Brother not to screw his life up more than necessary. He was in deep trouble, and he came to me. He may have helped solve the case. He solved part of it, at least."

"I didn't hear about that."

I told her. Her face was an interesting study as she listened. It went by subtle gradations from blank astonishment to red-hot anger, passing through denial, disbelief, and pain on the way.

When I finished, Wendy worked and sputtered for a few seconds before she could make words, and she made a few unladylike ones before saying, "Dammit, I *am* going to fire him. May I use the phone?"

"Will you let me talk for a minute?"

"Are you going to try to talk me out of this? It won't work. He could go to jail for this—who knows how it could make me look?"

"Your image," I said.

"If my image is going to be messed up, I'm the one who's going to do it," she said. "Besides, it's more than that. He *betrayed* me, Matt. He knew how much I hated Dinkover, but he opened the door for him. I'll never forgive Max for that—the only way I'll ever forgive him is if he really *did* kill the old bastard!"

"Shut up and listen for a minute," I said. Wendy scowled but subsided. "For one thing, Brother is being kept company right now at the DEA—Lieutenant Martin is the only outsider who's going to get a chance to talk to him."

"I'll call Network News and tell them," Wendy said. "I'll get the message across."

I ignored her. "For another thing, if Brother knows what's good for him, he's at this very moment spilling information that can put a serious crimp in the cocaine traffic. He can't do them any good if you disgrace him at this moment."

"Why not?"

"Because there is a good chance he will wind up dead within days."

"Give me a break, Matt."

"Try it, if you want him really punished." Wendy pouted but said nothing. "For a third thing," I went on, "he was *blackmailed* into letting Dinkover in. The way Brother saw it, he had no choice."

"You wouldn't have knuckled under," Wendy said.

"No, but Brother isn't as good a *person* as I am," I said. Wendy didn't even smile. "That was a joke," I told her.

"Ha, ha," she said, obliging me. "What do you want me to do, Matt?" she said. "Let him get away with it?"

"I don't want anybody to get away with anything. What I want you to do is a little blackmailing of your own."

"What's *that* supposed to mean?"

"It means the next time you can get to Brother, you tell him he's through, but you're willing to make it look amicable. He should take it like a lamb, contract or no contract. If he doesn't, you promise to take the case to the papers. That way you get rid of him without destroying him in the process."

"It sounds better than he deserves," she said.

"Yeah, but granting mercy is a luxury few people are in a position to experience. You might enjoy it."

Now she smiled. "All right, I'll give it a try." She scratched her chin. "You know, Max did do an awful lot for me. Financially, anyway. And that ex-wife of his is a real bitch . . ."

"I didn't ask you to *forgive* him, for God's sake," I protested.

"Don't worry. I'm just trying to convince myself that going easy on him is a good idea."

"Keep working on it," I told her. "I have to make a phone call." I picked up the receiver.

"Are you going out again? I heard something about that, too." When I told her she'd heard right, she said, "I wish you didn't have to."

"So do I," I told her, then turned and punched phone buttons.

When the Network night operator called, I told her to beep Al St. John for me, which she did with an alacrity that would have made Lieutenant Martin cry. I told her to have him call me when he reached her, then hung up the phone to wait.

Wendy had left the room while I dialed. I called to her, and she called back that she'd rejoin me in a few minutes.

The phone rang. I picked it up and told Al the bad news. He said Good Lord. "Bea Dunney is dead? Bea *Dunney?*" His voice cracked with the surprise of it.

"The cops have been trying to reach you at your place all day. I told you to get some sleep."

"I did," he said, "but I unplugged the phone. It still makes a ring the caller can hear when you do that, you know. After I woke up, I went to the movies. I didn't even look at a newspaper or anything. I was watching the movie when the beeper went off."

"I'm glad I finally reached you."

He still couldn't get over it. "Bea Dunney, Good Lord. Who would want to kill *her?*"

"Who would want to kill Wendy Ichimi?" I said it softly; Wendy had the knack for hearing things.

Al took this big, too. "Has something happened to Wendy, too?"

"No but just by luck. I'll tell you about it when I see you." I told him the police wanted to see us and gave him the address.

"Do you think this has something to do with the Dinkover case?"

I threw up my hands, then realized that was a pretty stupid way to communicate over the phone. "Who knows?" I said. "The cops think it might be, because they haven't been able to get in touch with the widow."

"What do *you* think, Matt?"

"I'm off thinking for a while," I told him. "There was a time I was convinced Harris's mugging had something to do with this. Then I went crazy over eagle stuff. I haven't been able to stop that, no matter how stupid it seems. Napoleon used eagles to symbolize his empire. I thought of that one this morning."

I could hear the smile in Al's voice. "You mean now we're looking for a Polish-American football player who—"

"Knock it off, Al, I'm not in the mood." Al wasn't noted for his sense of humor, but that topic really set him off. "I just want to point out where thinking has gotten me so far. I'll tell you more about the whole thing later. Now let's get over to Mrs. Dinkover's, it's getting late."

I hung up and went to the living room to find Wendy. She was wearing the nightgown I'd given her. She stood up and twirled around and said, "Ta-da," in a musical voice. "How do you like it?"

"What I like is you in it." That, of course, is the reason flannel is so much better than the other stuff. Soft fabric clings to soft flesh, revealing forms, leaving you to imagine the details. Or remember them. Either way is good.

"I just want to give you some incentive to hurry back," she said.

"Mission accomplished," I told her.

"Good," she said. She came to me and put her arms around me and kissed me. "Be careful, Matt," she said.

"You, too," I said sternly. I made her repeat the drill about not answering the phone and not opening the door for anybody but me.

"Don't worry, Matt," she said. "I'm not that brave."

"You're brave," I told her, "letting me see you in that nightgown."

She laughed, a very sexy laugh. We kissed again, and I left. I waited in the hall until I heard her throw the bolt and lock all the locks.

"Only a matter of time before people find out . . ."
—Christopher George, *The Immortal* (ABC)

CHAPTER FIFTEEN

I stepped outside to discover it had started to snow, and I smiled. We'd have a white Christmas, the first one since I couldn't remember when. Snow does something to New York. Yeah, I know, it snarls traffic and turns the city wet and disgusting gray with oily slush. But that all comes later; I'm talking about what happens while the snow is falling. It quiets the city, somehow, and softens the hard edges of the concrete. It's as if Nature wanted to show us no matter how big we build them, she can top them.

Snow also makes it difficult to walk in leather shoes. As I crossed the street, I had to walk flatfooted and plant my feet carefully. Just, I reminded myself grimly, as I had had to do when I crossed the ice toward Dinkover and the flag.

Snow does something else to New York—it makes the cabs disappear. I stood on the east side of Central Park West for a good six minutes waiting for one to come by.

The one I finally got was driven by a recent immigrant from Colombia, recent enough so that this was the first snow he'd ever seen. I could deduce all this from what he said: "Look at the *snow,* man. This never happen in Colombia."

It was an equally safe deduction that someone had impressed on him the idea that you should drive carefully in the snow. He kept both hands on the wheel and no feet on the accelerator. If that cab had been going any slower, it would have been backing up.

I think I may have propelled the taxi more with will power than the driver did with gasoline, but we eventually made it up to Eighty-first Street, across the Park, and down Fifth Avenue to the Dinkovers' building.

And after all that delay, I was astonished to find I was the first one there. I parked under the awning out of the snow to wait. Through the glass, the doorman gave me a suspicious look, but apparently I looked respectable enough to leave alone for a while. I smiled and waved at him and told him Merry Christmas, but it didn't seem to help.

I looked at snowflakes falling past a streetlamp to pass the time. The wind was blowing at just the right angle to make the illusion possible. You may have seen it yourself. You look at the flakes coming at you, lit up like stars, and suddenly they *are* stars, and they're not falling anymore, you are rising, soaring, zooming off. I discovered it when I was a kid, and got dismissed as a lunatic by a lot of people until I got Grover Balland to try it. Grover was the toughest kid in the neighborhood, and once he saw it, everybody was willing to try. And since it really works, I was suddenly a hero.

"Daydreaming?" said Al St. John.

I jumped. "Yes," I said, "that's exactly what I was doing." I toyed with the idea of telling him he could fly through space but decided against it. "How long have you been here?"

"Just got here. I took the Lexington Avenue subway and walked west. Um, I don't want to get out of line, Matt, but where are the cops?"

"Beats the hell out of me," I said.

"You know Lieutenant Martin better than I do . . ." he began.

I smiled. "Sometimes I know Lieutenant Martin better than *he* does."

"Well, is this the kind of thing he might do as a joke?"

I shook my head. "No way. He can be a joker, all right, but he doesn't joke about police work. The fact that he's not here yet can mean only one of two things. Either he's been delayed, by the weather or something else, or I screwed up his instructions."

That was the moment the lieutenant's unmarked car pulled up, accompanied by a blue and white unit and a wagon from the lab. Cops began to pile out of the vehicles. ADA Goosens emerged from the back seat of the lieutenant's car with a look on her face that said somebody is going to be sent to Mother Superior over *this*.

I don't know if it was the cops or the look on the Frying Nun's face, but something made the doorman decide it was time to come out. Before he could open his mouth, Lieutenant Martin reached inside his topcoat and pulled out a legal document. The doorman gave it a quick look, then pulled the door open and said, "This way, officers."

Livia Goosens led the way. Al and I followed with Lieutenant Martin.

"About time," I said pleasantly.

"If you're gonna be a clown," he said, "wear your goddamn makeup. There was a delay with the warrant. Then the Frying Nun got uppity with the judge, and we almost didn't get it at all."

He turned to Al. "St. John, where in hell have you been?"

Al filled him in, concluding, "And when Matt reached me, I headed right here. I don't even know what this is all about."

"That's okay—Cobb didn't tell you?" He looked at the two of us, trying to see in our faces if we had cooked something up. Apparently he convinced himself. "Bea Dunney was killed."

"I know that much, but that's all."

"That's okay, then. Your answers are that much more likely to be unbiased."

The elevator was done in gray enamel with white spots. Riding in it felt uncomfortably like being inside an oven.

When everyone was assembled in the carpeted white hallway on the ninth floor, the Frying Nun cleared her throat and told Rivetz he might begin.

Rivetz, who was going to begin the second the lieutenant got there in any case, gave her a dirty look and walked to the door. He knocked loudly, five times, then paused, then again five times.

"Mrs. Dinkover," he said. *"This is the police. We have a warrant to enter and search the premises."* He did some more knocking and some more yelling, with no response.

I noted with interest that Rivetz stood off to the side of the door itself while he was doing all this. It's a pleasure to watch a professional at work. This was the way it was supposed to be done. Maybe Carla Nelson Dinkover was not the most likely type to shoot a cop through a closed door, but too many cops had been shot by unlikely types for him to do it any other way.

Rivetz finished yelling, then looked a question at the lieutenant, who nodded in return. Rivetz stepped aside, and two muscular uniformed cops stepped up to the door.

Rivetz grinned at me. "Might as well let the young backs do the work, right?"

I learned something in the next few minutes. When the police have a warrant, and the desire to get in someplace, you can bet your grandmother's hearing aid they will get in. If they can't pick the lock (and very few people in burglary-conscious New York have pickable locks), they'll kick in the door. If you have a floor-lock deadbolt, and they can't kick in the door, they'll bust it open with an axe. That's what they did to the door of the Dinkover apartment. I don't know what they would have done if it had been a metal door too strong for an axe. Use a blowtorch, I guess. Dynamite.

Once the door gave in to the axe, Rivetz stuck his head through the opening and yelled again.

"Christ," I said, "if she didn't hear Officer Bunyan here chopping down the door, she must be dead."

The Frying Nun looked disgusted and told me to hold my tongue. I was tempted to take her literally and grab it with my hand. I get little urges like that sometimes—some kind of modified death wish. I usually manage to suppress them.

They dusted doorknobs for prints, then Rivetz reached through the hole in the door and unlocked it. Cops drew their guns and walked in, led by the Frying Nun. Nobody told me I had to stay out, so I gestured to Al St. John, and he and I brought up the rear. With six cops in front of us, we were the safest men in New York, unless we got attacked from behind.

The door opened into a hallway that ran the length of the apartment, with rooms opening off it on either side. Cops were opening doors, each time doing a condensed version of the routine Rivetz had gone through on the outside. I was looking at pictures.

The hallway walls were filled with pictures, both sides, from hip level to way above my head. It was hard to see wallpaper between them, there were so many. All of Dr. Paul Dinkover. A young Dinkover with

Jung; Dinkover with Einstein; Dinkover with Dr. Spock; Dinkover with Jerry Rubin; an angry Dinkover exchanging rude gestures with Nelson Rockefeller.

"I'm surprised he hung that one up," I said to Al.

"Why's that?"

"Scandalous. Dr. Dinkover reverting to symbolic behavior."

It was a big apartment. Farther down, the hallway turned a corner, and the cops were working there now. Not wishing to press my luck, I stayed and looked at pictures.

There was one picture I looked at a long time. It was one of the smaller pictures, an old glossy black and white snapshot. It showed Dr. Dinkover with his arm around a smaller man, an Oriental man. In his other arm, Dinkover holds a little girl, also Oriental. The men are smiling, the girl is not. She is reaching with both arms across Dinkover's body toward the other man, who doesn't see her. If that's not a picture of Henry Ichimi and Wendy, I decided, I will eat it. I could find out for sure, of course, by asking Wendy. I didn't think that was much of an idea, though.

About then, one of the cops reported finding a fully equipped darkroom. That cleared up a few minor mysteries. Carla Dinkover had been a journalist—no reason why she shouldn't have been interested in photography as well. It also explained the gallery. She had probably taken a lot of these pictures, and, on the evidence of the darkroom, developed them as well.

Al St. John had a frightened look on his face.

"What's the matter?" I demanded.

"Is anything wrong? You look like you're in pain."

"Pain?"

"You know. It's the look you get before you get—get a big idea."

That was interesting. I'd never known I did that. "Very perceptive of you. I am getting an idea. The pain is because I don't like it."

"What do you mean?"

"Whoever killed Bea Dunney—whoever was *trying* to kill Wendy—used DMSO mixed with cyanide."

"So?"

"So I heard the cops speculating on the most likely source of cyanide. Photographic chemicals."

"Oh," Al said. "Ohh. And you think—"

I was about to tell him I didn't know what to think when we were interrupted by a cop's voice from around the corner.

"Lieutenant! Ms. Goosens! Over here."

I heard footsteps and grumbling. Then I heard a curse from Lieutenant Martin and a shriek from the Frying Nun. The shriek was kind of endearing—made her seem more human.

A split second later, I realized my brain had only thought that to disguise from me the fact that I had secretly decided to go see what the fuss was about. I told Al to wait, then strode through that long hallway, and not one cop said a word about it. Maybe Ms. Goosens was right about my hanging around too much.

I was even more inclined to agree with her when I rounded the corner and reached the room.

It was a study, the leather chair and book-lined wall kind. A rack of pipes. That kind of place. The only modern touch was the IBM personal computer on the desk. Dinkover (and/or his wife—she was a writer, too) undoubtedly used it as a word processor, because there was a top-quality daisy wheel printer with it and, next to that, a neat stack of paper perforated for a drive wheel.

And on the floor was the body of Carla Nelson Dinkover. There was a wet spot on the dark blue plush carpeting and an empty glass near her hand, but on the whole she had died much more neatly than her husband had.

It was still ugly. Her body was still youthful, still looked as if it could spring out of that awkward and ungraceful position any time, and be back charming and alluring as ever. But her face would never charm anyone again. For one thing, the reason they call it *cyan*ide is that it turns you blue. From asphyxiation, as your muscles cease to make your lungs and heart work.

Lieutenant Martin told Rivetz to call the morgue.

"For God's sake—be careful out there!"
—Michael Conrad, *Hill Street Blues*
(NBC)

CHAPTER SIXTEEN

The note had been written on the computer; it was still attached to the stack that had been threaded through the printer.

"*. . . sorry for the trouble I caused,*" it said in part, "*but there was nothing else I could do. I loved Paul Dinkover, but Paul Dinkover was a* mind, *a mind that will come to be recognized as the greatest of this century. That mind was slipping away from him. There is nothing sadder than the senility of a great man. I could not watch him struggle uselessly against dotage, incontinence, death. I owed it to the man I loved to do it now, to save him that losing battle.*"

All in all, it was quite a document. It told us that Mrs. Dinkover had accompanied her husband to the Blades Club that night; how he had let her in after Max Brother had admitted him; how she took the knife and did it. She chose the Blades Club, the printout said, because she wanted to embarrass Wendy Ichimi.

There was a whole lot of stuff about Wendy. How she had become an obsession with the old man. How he had tried to lead her to a sane life, how she had refused to let go of the unhealthy and alien symbols by which she tried to be American, and how she hated him for it. How, in the end, she had laughed at him.

"*I decided embarrassing her would not be enough. Being involved in a murder investigation would be inconvenient, nothing more. My work would not be finished as long as she remained alive. I am firmly convinced that concern for this insensitive wretch caused Paul's condition to deteriorate. She has deprived mankind of his genius; for that, I have killed her."*

The note concluded by saying Mrs. Dinkover had erased the computer memory and destroyed all the copies of her husband's manuscript. It was gibberish, the note said, and would tarnish the great man's reputation. Finally, it had some instructions for the disposition of the estate.

"Well?" I said.

"Well, what?" Lieutenant Martin countered, pushing me away. "You know I hate it when you read over my shoulder."

"Bullshit," I said amiably. "You've known I was here all along. You wanted me to read the note. If you didn't, you would have shoved me off right away. Or, more likely, you would have left me twiddling my thumbs in the parlor with Al St. John, the way I've been doing for three hours. I might as well be under arrest."

To be fair, I hadn't spent the whole three hours twiddling my thumbs. I spent a fair amount of time answering questions for the Frying Nun. She seemed to be convinced that I had known what they were going to find here. She didn't go so far as to suggest that I had arranged it. I spent some time listening to them question Al St. John about the possible switching of the DMSO this morning, but no one seemed to have his heart much in that operation. Al couldn't tell them much anyway, except it was perfectly possible for Mrs. Dinkover to have done that, and we knew that already.

For the second time that day, I watched lab boys coming and going. And, after pleading failed, reason foundered, and threats got pretty nasty, I was allowed to call Wendy. I wasn't allowed to *tell* her anything ("Something's come up; I don't know how long I'll be gone, bye."), but at least she knew I was alive. A moral victory.

I'd gone back to twiddling; after a while Lieutenant Martin sent for me with some hot air about wanting to look at the death room to make sure they got the position of the body right. When I got there, he mumbled something, then cleared the decks for me to see the note.

Now he was giving me a look pregnant, as the saying goes, with meaning, without actually giving birth to anything intelligible.

"Don't you ever, Matty," he said, "tell anybody I showed you that note. You can think what you like, and I can't pull it out of your head or anything, but you were never supposed to see it."

"Got you, Mr. M.," I said.

He was foxy, now. "But seeing as how you *have* read it," he said, "what do you think?"

I raised a brow. "I think it's pretty irrelevant what I think."

"Don't be modest, boy."

I shrugged. "It's my nature," I told him and pretended not to notice when he snorted. "Besides," I went on, "it doesn't make any difference. Even as we speak, the Frying Nun is out in the hallway telling reporters from all the papers, and I hope the Network, that this wraps up the case."

"She's not." The lieutenant's jaw had dropped so far it looked as if he would have to push it back into place with his hands.

"Sorry. I take it you think she's being a little premature."

He made a noise. "Yeah, a little. Do I have to line it out for you?"

"I don't think so. I saw a few holes in the computer paper note that weren't made with a punch. The question is, what are you going to do about it?"

By golly, the lieutenant *did* push his jaw back in place with his hand, in the act of rubbing his chin to help him think. "That's the question all right. What *can* I do about it?"

"Bitch to the commissioner," I suggested.

"Hell, I've done that already; don't do any good." He smacked his fist into his palm. "Dammit, if she wasn't such a smart goddam lawyer, she wouldn't brown me off so much when she does these things."

He started walking around the room, using some arcane cop radar to avoid the taped outline on the floor without even looking down.

"I can't run out there and tell the reporters she's full of what the birds eat," he said. "Much as I'd like to. Wouldn't do any good anyway, except make us both look foolish."

" 'COPS AND DA BICKER ON SHRINK WIDOW SUICIDE,' " I said.

"Exactly." The lieutenant sighed. "All I can do is let her rave, and keep the case open on my own."

"Doing what?"

"Taking a nice long hard look at the suicide here. If that's what it is."

"If that's what it is," I echoed. "Can I go home?"

The lieutenant laughed at that. "Sure, if the case is wrapped up, who needs you? You know, Matty, the bitch of it is, all the objections we see could easily be explained away. No reason the Frying Nun can't be one hundred percent right. But go on, get the hell out of here. Take your pal with you."

I rose to go. The lieutenant said, "Keep in touch, Matty."

I said, "Didn't you get my Christmas card?" and left him.

In the elevator on the way downstairs, Al St. John and I decided it would be impossible to find two cabs on a night like this and damn near impossible to find even one. We'd walk uptown through the snow and take the bus across the park on Seventy-ninth Street—then he could get a subway and I would walk down Central Park West home.

I turned up my collar. The snow made cold kisses on my face. I stuck my gloveless hands deep in my pockets against the chill. I kept telling myself it meant a white Christmas, but it wasn't enough. I had to talk to keep my mind off my misery.

I briefed Al about the contents of the note, gave him a minute or two to digest it, then asked him what he thought.

"It stinks," he said. It was still snow-quiet in the city. Al's voice sounded strange, as if we were in some sort of echo-deadening room.

Time to play Devil's advocate. "What's wrong with it?"

"Well, in the first place, why did she do a suicide note on the computer?"

"Why not? It was in the house. Her husband used it; maybe she did too."

"It's convenient, though, isn't it, Matt? They can compare handwriting; and they can even tell from the touch on a typewriter—even an electric—exactly who did the typing. But Good Lord, Matt, everything that comes out of a daisy wheel printer is going to look exactly the same."

I looked at him. That was one I hadn't even thought of. "Good work," I told him. "If there were a habitual misspelling, or an obvious stylistic quirk, we might get an indication. But it wouldn't be legal evidence. Okay, what else?"

"If she had easy access to so much poison, why did she have to stab her husband? If what the note says is right, she killed him out of love. Why did she choose such a painful way of doing it?"

We crossed Seventy-ninth Street and stood under the bus shelter on the corner. I looked down the street for the bus, but visibility in the snow was near zero.

"Go on," I said.

"Okay, Matt, how about this? How did she know Wendy used DMSO? She had to know that in order to switch the bottles, but how could she have found out?"

"It's no secret," I said, playing Devil's advocate again.

"It's not exactly common knowledge. And how did she turn up at Brother's office? If Carla Dinkover was the killer, her story of an anonymous phone call falls apart."

"Maybe she was following Wendy, just waiting for a chance to switch bottles—this is assuming she knew, of course—and barged into Brother's office because she'd seen the rest going in and wanted a handy group of suspects. Or maybe she didn't do anything at Brother's office; she showed up there as a red herring, then made the switch in the crowd outside the Garden."

"Good Lord, Matt, you don't really believe that?"

"Good Lord, Al, of course I don't. I have all your objections and more. But the lieutenant's right—the objections don't *have* to mean anything. What's keeping the damn bus?"

I turned and looked down the road again. I started nibbling my thumb until my hand got too cold, then I shoved it back in my pocket.

Al said, "Maybe we just missed one before we got here," and I grunted noncommittally. Then he said, "What did I miss?"

A car skidded quietly out of control into the intersection, like something in a slow-motion comedy. The driver regained control, and the car moved on.

"What did I miss, Matt?"

"Nothing, except the M-17 bus," I told him.

Just then the big black-windowed bus pulled up as if answering to its name. I realized with a shock of embarrassment that I didn't have exact change, a *faux pas* a native New Yorker should never commit, but Al made up the difference, and we got on, moving to a seat in the rear.

We were pretty much alone—apparently most people had decided to stay home, or maybe get to where they were going by ski.

"It can't be nothing," Al said.

"What can't be nothing?" I caught my reflection in the dark-tinted glass across the bus. I looked like the world's most unfortunate dandruff sufferer; I began brushing fat snowflakes from my hair.

"What I missed about that note. You said you had all my objections and more."

"So what?"

"If you have more objections, I must have missed something, right?"

I shook my head. More snow came off. "Not at all," I said. "You weren't there when Mrs. Dinkover gave me the big sell about her husband's forthcoming masterwork, how the part he'd already finished —the introduction and the stuff about religious symbolism—would make a Third Testament in and of themselves. Except that she led one to believe her husband's book would make the previous two testaments obsolete.

"This," I said, "is the drivel she supposedly burned and bulk-erased from the computer this afternoon."

"Maybe she was stringing you along, Matt. Putting up a good front."

"Your turn to play Devil's advocate now, huh?"

He grinned. "I guess so. But I mean it. If she'd already killed her husband, she would naturally have been putting on an act."

"Maybe so, but if she were, she had no reason to commit suicide. She was the greatest actress who ever lived. She *glowed* with fervor, Al, it was incredible. She had me convinced the book *would* be great, and I was hardly a Dinkover fan.

"And you should have seen her with her 'who let my husband in' business. All she had to do was parade that in front of a jury, and they would have believed anything. She was fanatically devoted to her husband."

"Exactly," Al said.

The bus fishtailed a little on the curviest part of the traverse across the Park. The bus driver called back a cheerful, "Sorry!" and slowed down a little.

"Let me finish," I said to Al. "She was fanatically devoted to her husband, but with him gone, the fanaticism was transferred to his work and to finding out who killed him. If I'm wrong about that, I'll go live in a cave and eat berries."

"Well," Al said, "only you know what she looked and acted like."

We rode in silence until the bus stopped for a light at the corner of Central Park West and Eighty-first Street (the traverse doesn't go straight through the park, it curves a little), when I said to Al, "You want to know what's really driving me nuts?"

"The fact that you still have to go home and walk the dog?"

"Great!" I said. I had forgotten all about that. That meant I had to stay in these cold wet shoes a little longer. Al started to smile. "Laugh and you die," I told him.

He laughed, but I was too miserable to kill him. The light changed; the bus crossed the intersection and stopped. Al and I got off the bus and stood in the snow.

"There's something else driving me nuts," I said.

"What's that?"

"All right. Say the note we found is gospel. Say Dinkover was losing the battle with Father Time, and his wife couldn't stand to watch. Say she knifed him and got Bea Dunney in an attempt at Wendy—" I had a sudden thought and broke off.

"Here's another objection," I said. "Carla Dinkover decided she was going to punch her own ticket when her work was done, right?"

"That's the theory," Al said.

"Okay. Why didn't she wait until the job was *done*, for God's sake? All she had to do was listen to the radio; we've got two all-news stations. She could have taken her choice. As soon as she hears Wendy's gone, *then* she could gargle cyanide. If it misfired, as it did, she'd be alive to fight another day."

"You're right," Al said. "But go on with what you were saying."

"Yeah. All right, say she was overconfident. We can concede every little thing we want, but when we do, we're left with one little question."

"What's that?"

"Why did he go for the flag?" I said. "Why did he go for the flag? Why did he grab the goddamn eagle?"

Al said nothing. He looked stunned. The way I felt.

"Got any answers?" I asked.

"Maybe . . . maybe it was just an anti-government thing, like the lieutenant thought."

I smiled a sad smile. "The lieutenant never thought that, and you don't either, any more than I do."

"You are so right," he said.

I told him I'd see him tomorrow. I watched him walk around the newsstand to the subway entrance, then turned and headed downtown.

This was worse than the walk to the bus stop had been, because I was heading into the wind, and the snow was hitting me in the face. It's amazing how something that looks so soft and fluffy can be so gritty when it lands in your eye.

I kept my head down and tried to keep my mind off my troubles by trying to decide how I was going to talk Wendy into doing what I wanted her to do. This was a particularly absorbing topic, because I still wasn't sure what I wanted her to do.

Because now I was trusting my instincts. I wasn't buying that computer-generated suicide note. Somebody had set this all up, killing Mrs. Dinkover by poisoning her drink. The note was supposed to be the ribbon on the nice neat package for the police.

It would be a tempting package. This was a high-publicity case; the cops were getting a lot of flak. Even if they weren't too crazy about all the details, that confession would make a nice out. It would even, I realized, make a nice smoke screen—pretend to have accepted the story the note offered, then carry on a nice, trouble-free investigation.

That, I decided, was probably what the Frying Nun had had in mind. She was too smart to have gone for the note so quickly otherwise. I gave her a grudging mental apology, then forgot her. She wasn't my problem.

My problem was, what's the safest thing for Wendy to do? If the killer was finished (and the note made it look that way), the best thing to do would be to get things back to normal immediately. Let him (or her) feel safe, and maybe he would be content to stay retired. If we were to act as if we didn't believe the note, he might get scared, and scared people are dangerous people. Especially ones who have shown three times they don't mind knocking off somebody inconvenient.

But. On the other hand. What if the killer considers Wendy unfinished business? What if he decides the note was a nice try, but it would have to be sacrificed to get the job done? Then it would be madness to let Wendy skate tomorrow. Criminal. There would be no excuse for it.

Unless you wanted to set a trap.

I stopped in my tracks and shook myself. Where the hell had that one come from? I wanted to slap myself in the face—sure, it rankled that we were no closer to our pal than we were when he horned in on Network business to kill Dinkover, but that didn't give me the right to get so brave all of a sudden with Wendy's pretty neck.

I grumbled at myself all the way back to my building. I was glad to see it. I waved hello to the doorman and started for the elevators.

"Hold it a second, Mr. Cobb," he said. "Package for you."

"For me?" I asked stupidly, then, "Oh. Thanks."

It was a bag from the neighborhood's intellectual bookstore. They deliver, which is nice, but I don't deal with them much because they have such a lousy mystery section. I certainly hadn't ordered anything from them today.

The bag had my name written on it, though, and my address and apartment number. I looked inside and saw a package, gift-wrapped. The way things had been going, my first instinct was to go out and bury it in the snow, but I decided I might as well ask Wendy about it first.

I took the elevator to the eighteenth floor, which is really the seventeenth floor, a fact which never fails to irritate me, and went over and rang the doorbell of the Sloans' apartment.

Spot started his happy bark as soon as I did. That was a good sign. Another good sign was that the next thing I heard was the peephole thing being opened. I stepped back—those things aren't built to look at tall people through—and wanted Wendy to be good and sure it was me.

Chain bolts were undone, locks slid open, and the door opened. Wendy, still sexy and beautiful in the nightgown, took a look at me and started to laugh.

"What's so funny?" I demanded. I stepped inside, closed the door behind me, and redid the locks.

"You look like a snowman," she said.

"I'd hate to tell you what I feel like."

"Oh, poor Matt. You'll feel better once you get out of those wet things." Right, I thought, and into your arms. She found a dry spot on my cheek and gave me a kiss.

"I sure will," I said. "Unfortunately, I have to walk Spot first."

"Give me a few minutes, and I'll be right with you."

"You will not. You will stay right here with the door locked."

Wendy's black eyes were shiny with excitement. "Matt, it doesn't matter now. Haven't you heard the news? I thought that's where you were."

"I was there."

"Then what's the matter? It's over, isn't it?"

"I wouldn't bet on it."

"It has to be over. I heard a woman say it on the radio. They interrupted the Christmas carols. I called Ivan and told him everything would be okay—I'll be ready to skate again by tomorrow evening. He passed it on to the Ice-Travaganza people and the Network."

I looked at her. I was thinking I could have saved myself all the soul searching on the way home.

"For the special. You know, the Network. You work there. I have a contract. You made me pregnant last night. Matt, for God's sake, say something."

"Call them back. Tell them you've changed your mind."

"I can't do that. Not now. I've already told everybody."

"It could be dangerous."

"What the hell are you *talking* about? It's *over*. She was as crazy as *he* was, and they canceled each other out, and now I'm free. Matt, what is the matter?"

I told her, in detail. Wendy took it stoically, nodding her head from time to time to show she understood.

". . . so I don't know what to tell you," I concluded. "I could be seeing things that aren't there, and even if they are there, it's a coin flip as to what's the best thing to do."

"There's something you left out," she said.

"What?"

"I'm not saying I believe you, now," she warned. "Those objections of yours seem pretty nitpicky, to me."

"It doesn't feel right," I insisted. "Those little things add up."

"Having it over with feels right to me," Wendy said. "I want it to be Dinkover's wife. I want that so bad."

"Wendy, for Christ's sake—"

"But even if you're right. Somebody's out there determined to kill me."

"Maybe."

"That's not very comforting, Matt."

"I know. Best I can do, though."

"That's my point," she said, then her face folded up, and her eyes got heavy with tears. "The best you can do isn't going to be enough. If I don't skate tomorrow, okay, but I can't stay here the rest of my life."

Spot always investigates when he sees a woman crying. He rested his snout on Wendy's lap and looked up at her with sympathetic eyes. She scratched his ears absently as she went on.

"If he really wants to get me, sooner or later, he will. Won't he?"

I couldn't make myself say anything.

"That answers the question, I think," Wendy said. "So if I skate tomorrow, you and the police set something up so that if he tries to kill me, you catch him."

"Just like that, huh?"

"Do the best you can," she said, then smiled.

"You want to use yourself as bait," I told her.

"I want it *over with*. I don't want to die; I just want this over with. Don't tell me you didn't think of it yourself."

"I thought of it. I didn't like it much."

"What would you do if you were in my position?"

I thought it over and decided I would skate. Not from any great courage; I just really resent the idea that some murdering son of a bitch is going to have me rearranging my life. Wendy wasn't crying, now, and I could see a lot of the same attitude in her face. I was surprised, but I shouldn't have been. You don't get to be the best in the world at anything without plenty of what my grandmother used to call Moxie. I told Wendy what I would do was irrelevant. She jeered at me for ducking the question, but I felt guilty enough without actively encouraging her.

I called Spot over and hooked the lead to his collar. Then I told Wendy to lock up behind me and went to the door.

"Are you going to take the package back outside with you?" she asked.

I had forgotten all about it. "Oh. No. What the hell is this thing?"

"Your Christmas present. I got the idea from your mother."

"Oh, for God's sake."

Wendy giggled. "Possibly," she said. "I called the bookstore and had them deliver it—found them in the Yellow Pages. Some things about New York are really great."

"Fabulous," I said. "Now nobody knows you're here except everybody who works for the bookstore and all the customers."

"Matt," she said reproachfully. "There is more to me than just the Japanese-American neato cutesy bouncy cheerleader you seem to think I am. I didn't give them my *name*. I put it on a credit card I've got—"

"And you didn't give them your name? Let alone your account number and, God help us, expiration date?"

"The credit card is in *Max's* name. He got me one just so I could buy stuff without having a fuss made. And I didn't even have them bring it up to the apartment, did I? They left it with the doorman."

"Oh," I said. "Sounds okay. I apologize. What is it?"

"Oh, no. Do not open until Christmas. Or at least Christmas Eve."

"Oh, all right," I said. I opened the door. "You didn't have to."

"I wanted to." She stood on tiptoe and gave me a soft kiss. "Hurry back," she said.

Spot got excited the moment he saw the snow. He was straining at his leash, something he hardly ever does. The doorman said, "He's a lot more eager to go out there than I am."

"Well," I said, "he hasn't been walked since this afternoon. Also, it's genetic. He was bred to be a sled dog; when he sees snow, he goes all ethnic on me."

It wasn't snowing quite as hard now, but it was colder. Most of the doormen in this classy neighborhood had conscientiously shoveled sidewalks, so the walking wasn't so bad. I told Spot to make it quick, but he was having none of it. He was going crazy with repressed friskiness. After I tugged him back for about the third time, he looked up at me with these big cow eyes he makes. I was cold enough and wet enough to have smacked him if he whimpered at me, but Spot was too smart for that. He just looked soulful.

"All right, goddammit," I said as I bent to let him off the lead, "but stay in sight." I reflected, as I watched him jump in and out of snow drifts, and generally frolic, that he could stay in plain sight and still disappear if he wanted to. All he had to do was lie down in the snow, close his eyes, and cover his little black nose with one paw. I read somewhere that polar bears hunt that way.

Spot sprinted down the block, then turned around to see what was keeping me. He seemed disappointed that I wasn't as enthusiastic about the whole business as he was.

I called to him to stay, and his expensive obedience training was never put to a tougher test. He gave me that soulful look again, but my heart was frozen solid. I told him again to stay, and he did. He rolled around the snow a few times, and made a few experimental jumps, but he remained in more or less the same spot. I was proud of him.

The next thing to do was to get him to come back to me. This would be easier—it would give him a chance to sprint a good half block through the snow, and I doubted he'd resist that. I opened my mouth to give the command, but I was jumped before I could do it.

Footsteps on fresh snow make no noise. The first inkling I had that I was under attack came when I felt the thump in my back.

Actually, it was something more than a thump. It was a flying tackle that knocked the breath from me and sent me sprawling face first into a snowdrift.

I tried to roll over, to be able to fight back, but when I did, my eyes were full of snow and I was blind. Before I could clear them, my attacker was on top of me. A vertical right cross to my chin turned me back over. My head was buried in a snow drift. When I tried to open my eyes again, all I could see was stars against a field of white.

I thrashed and struggled and did similar useless things. My attacker never said anything (not that I could hear too well in any case); he just pressed his knee against my spine until I was sure he was going to crack it.

I was struggling now, even more desperately. Struggling for air. I couldn't free my face from the snow, not even a nostril. I couldn't even melt an airway for myself with my breath, because the son of a bitch who was riding my back kept forcing my face deeper into the snow. The field of white was becoming a field of dark red, and my mind was starting to race. I was going to die, this bastard was going to drown me, I was going to drown right here on West Seventy-third Street, between Central Park West and Columbus Avenue, and he would bury me in a snowbank and nobody would find me till spring. My last thought before the roaring in my ears became too loud for me to hear myself think was that here was the first White Christmas in years, and I was going to miss it . . .

Then I felt his hand in my pocket. The one where I keep bus change. Subway tokens. And my keys.

I had a vision of Wendy, happy Wendy, loving Wendy, rushing to take the chain bolt off when she heard the key in the lock.

The roaring in my ears got louder.

CHAPTER SEVENTEEN

I would have cursed myself, if I could have opened my mouth. As it was, I just got mad. The struggling I was doing was worse than useless. Lucky Pierre up there had all the leverage—all I was doing was exhausting myself, killing myself that much sooner.

I had to devote the few remaining molecules of oxygen in my brain to *thinking*. So I tried to think, and what do you know, it worked.

I did one last thrash and brought my arms up so that my hands were near my face. Then I stopped moving. I didn't expect my assailant to get off me—I just wanted to get him to relax a little.

I don't know if he did or not. I just waited until I couldn't stand it any more, then I moved. I planted my hands (cold beyond feeling now) against the asphalt beneath the snow and pushed straight back. I lifted myself (and my friend) only a couple of inches, but it was enough. It changed angles, leverages. Now I could use my legs.

Before I could get forced back down into the snow, I pulled my legs up flat, knees out, like a frog. Then, with whatever purchase I could get against the snow and the slick pavement below it, I leaped.

It worked better than I thought—the man on my back had just shifted his weight toward my head to force me back down after my push-up—my frog maneuver just encouraged him to keep going.

I didn't quite do a flip—I got up about sixty degrees, then went over sideways. The important thing was, I had him off my back, and after I spat a two-pound lump of snow from my mouth, I could breathe again. Cold air never tasted so good.

It was nice to breathe, but I knew my troubles weren't over by a long shot. I still couldn't see. I rubbed my eyes with my left hand, while I kept my right extended to try to ward off another attack.

Which never came.

As I pulled air by the bushel into my lungs, the roaring in my ears subsided enough for me to hear why. Spot was at my side, snarling and barking. I was going to give him the kill command, but he stopped doing it, which meant my attacker was out of sight.

I got one eye functioning well enough to see the line of indistinct footprints leading out of sight around the corner.

I stood there, panting and squinting and trying to fight off the world with one hand. Then I took a deep breath and collapsed, falling on my ass in the snow.

Spot came over and started to lick my face, and for the first time in my life, I actually enjoyed it. It was warm and rough, and it started to bring me back to life.

"Where the hell were you?" I demanded when I had enough breath to talk.

Spot cocked his head and said, *"Moooort?"* which is how a Samoyed expresses concern. I reached out and gave him a hug. I knew what had taken him so long. He thought I was frolicking in the snow with a friend. When he got the message I was in trouble, he came right to my rescue. God bless him.

I caught my breath at last and struggled to my feet. I put my hands in my pockets against the cold. No keys.

No change or subway tokens, for that matter. I screamed and dropped to my knees. Spot was startled, but I could apologize to him later. At Wendy's funeral, for instance.

I swept my hands through the snow, frantic until I found the keys. Spot had scared him off before he had a good grip on them. Or the attack had been a simple mugging, and he hadn't especially been after my keys at all. Shades of Harris Brophy. I was getting damn sick of this case.

Wendy didn't even wait until the door was opened. Right after she looked through the peephole, she said, "Matt, my God! What happened?"

She didn't wait to hear an answer before she opened the door, for which I was grateful. I stumbled in and said, "Take Spot's leash off—my fingers are too stiff. Meet me in the extra bathroom."

I couldn't help seeing myself in the bathroom mirror. Grisly. Bright red where I wasn't frozen white. I got some warm water running in the sink and put my hands under it. I knew it would hurt, but I didn't know it was going to hurt that much. Still, it worked. With the pain came (some) flexibility. I started to peel off my stiff, sodden clothes. What wasn't crusted with snow was soaked with sweat.

Wendy came in and joined me. "I know I'm repeating myself, but you've got to expect that if you don't answer questions. What happened to you? From the bruises on your back, it looks like you got run over by a snowplow."

"Not that simple. Did anyone try to get in here?"

"Nope. All alone, just me and the radio. Look, Matt, if you don't want to tell me, just say so."

I told her all about it, emphasizing the attempt to get my keys. I concluded by saying, "Still want to skate tomorrow?"

We went around with that one for a while. The conclusion was that this didn't really change anything, except to make it more likely we'd have somebody to look for tomorrow.

By now I was naked. The clothes were in a heap in the tub. I couldn't think of any better place for them, so I padded into the other bathroom and started the water running. I was just about to step in to the shower, when I had a sudden thought. I said a rude word, told the shower not to go away, and went to the other room to inform the police about my little adventure.

Lieutenant Martin was impressed. Bewildered, but impressed. He asked me if I was okay, and that taken care of, he asked me what I thought. It's a misdemeanor to use on the telephone the words it would have taken to describe what I thought, so I skipped it. Lieutenant Martin said he'd be at the Garden tomorrow, along with as many men as he could spare. And maybe some police women so that the female skaters' locker room could be watched too.

I said it sounded like a good idea and told him I'd have as many of my people there as I could get, for what it was worth. Then he griped to me about the case, and I stayed on the phone, but the whole time I was fantasizing about the shower. My body had thawed out to the point where it wouldn't hurt any more, it would just feel great.

Finally, it was okay to hang up. I did so with glee, then headed for the bathroom. Someone was humming in the shower stall.

I was crushed. "Aw, Wendy," I said. Now I had to go to the other bathroom and shlep all the disgusting wet clothes somewhere else . . .

The shower door opened. Wendy was smiling under the spray, rubbing her self vigorously with a washcloth, and generally disporting herself like an incredibly sexy seal.

"Well, come *on*," she said. "You wanted to get warm, didn't you?"

"Oh," I said. "Sure." I joined her under the spray. We helped each other wash those hard-to-reach places.

"Hey," I said, "this really works."

Wendy pushed wet hair from her eyes. "Getting warm?"

"Can't you tell?" I took her in my arms.

"Matt," she said, "stay with me tomorrow."

"Every second," I promised, "except when you're on the ice."

She held me tighter. "Good. Good. That's what I want."

After that we didn't talk for a while.

Of course, my staying with Wendy next day meant she had to stay with me—I had a few errands to do, and I had to put in at least an appearance at the Network.

Before we left the apartment that morning, Wendy slipped the package into my coat pocket.

"Open it when I'm on the ice," she said.

"So during the only time I won't be next to you, I'll be thinking of you?"

"Matt, you're so *romantic*. Actually, it's so I'm out of reach if you don't like it."

"What is it, a bomb, for God's sake?"

"No. But your mother ought to get a kick out of it, too, if you use it properly."

"It's a cookbook," I said, but Wendy just said wait and see.

The first thing on the agenda was to get myself a pair of gloves, which I did on the way to the Network. Black leather, with rabbit fur inside, warm and soft. I made a promise to remember not to bleed inside the goddam things. When we went back outside, it was a pleasure not to have to keep my hands in my pockets all the time.

I visited the Network next, using the phone to tell my people I'd need them tonight. They all signed on, including Al, who was especially eager. I told him to call Lieutenant Martin and work out details, then get back to our staff.

"Who's in?" he said.

"Everybody. You, Kolaski, Smith, Ragusa, me."

"What about Shirley?" he said. "Nobody's seen her in days."

"She's been at the hospital. I'm going to ask her in person. I want to see Harris, anyway. Going to compare notes." I told him how I'd almost wound up with two lungfuls of snow.

"Good Lord, Matt," he said. "This guy must be a maniac."

"If the attack on me is connected at all," I said.

"Too many coincidences," he said. "One or two, okay, but this is too many."

"You know something?"

"What?"

"I agree with you one hundred percent."

"You're a good teacher," he said. "I try to think the way you think."

"Yeah, well you still can't have a raise. I'll be at the hospital. If you need me, beep me."

Harris was making a remarkable recovery, and Shirley acted as if she had spent three days witnessing a miracle. She met me and Wendy at the entrance of the hospital, and spent the whole walk up to Harris's room telling us the good news.

"The doctor says he's going to make a complete recovery. As soon as all his bones heal, he'll be good as new. Of course, he'll be a little weak, but they said no brain damage, no nerve damage. It'll be a month or so before he leaves the hospital, naturally, and longer than that before he can come back to work, but it's still pretty wonderful."

"It is," I said. "Especially considering the way he looked that first night."

"I'm glad," Wendy said. "I like Harris a lot."

Shirley was so happy she didn't even give Wendy a dirty look.

Leaving aside the bandages and the traction sling and the purple spots on his face, Harris was pretty much his old chipper self.

"Shirley's been telling us the good news," I said.

"Shirley *is* the good news," he replied. Shirley blushed, no surprise. "Do you know she's been here practically every second since I was brought to the hospital? She's eaten here, slept here, in the waiting room down the hall. Only time she was away was when I sent her away, and when she went with you to check out my apartment."

"We got there too late," I said. "Sorry."

Harris tried to shrug, winced, and laughed. "Reflexes are stupid. I've been trying to shrug for three days now, and it hurts every time. Don't worry about the apartment, Matt. I've got insurance. I'll miss the coin collection, though. My father started it."

This was rare. I'd never heard Harris speak of his family before. In fact, Harris was so cool and detached, it was hard to imagine him even *having* a family. He'd always struck me as the kind of person who'd never been a child—not dignified enough.

"Anyway," Harris said, "when I finally came out of my haze, there she was. She's a hell of a woman, isn't she?" Another blush.

"I keep telling you that," I said.

"Maybe I better start listening." He moved his eyes over toward Wendy. She took a step to her left so he could see her better. "I've spent the last day or so bringing myself up to date on your problems, Wendy," Harris said. "Ordinarily, I'd be at the Network, telling Matt what to do, and things would be all settled by now."

I laughed. "We've hardly noticed you were gone."

"St. John doing a good job?"

"Incredible. I don't know when he sleeps."

"He wants your job," Harris said. "He's been studying you since he signed on. He's too goddam eager."

"He's too smart for that, I hope. You know, Harris," I said, "*I* got mugged last night."

Shirley looked surprised. Harris looked at me and said, "Well, you came through it in a lot better shape than I did."

"Maybe he couldn't find a pipe."

"Wrench," Harris said. "He did me with a wrench. Maybe he

couldn't find one, at that. But the m.o. is too different, Matt. Even if it was the same guy, you'd never be able to prove it. I don't think these things are connected anyway."

"Still a funny coincidence, though," Wendy said.

Harris looked at her for a second, then ran his tongue around the inside of his mouth before answering. It made his bandages jump on his head. "There are plenty of muggers in New York, Wendy," he said quietly. "If a person lives long enough, he's likely to be the victim of a crime sooner or later. Matt and I have been lucky enough to have survived ours."

Wendy blanched. I tightened the screws on my self-control, hard. If I hadn't, Harris might have found himself nursing a few new broken bones.

"Wendy," I said, "I want to talk to Harris for a couple of minutes about Network stuff. Bore you to death. Why don't you and Shirley step into the hall for a few minutes."

Then I remembered my promise to be by her side every second and added, "Don't go away or anything. Just stand right by the window in the door so I can see you, okay? Shirley is just as good a conversationalist as I am."

"Better," Harris said. I gave him a dirty look. His help I didn't need at the moment.

Wendy, after an initial twinge, seemed to take it fine. She gave me a little smile and said, "Sure, Matt." Her good-bye to Harris was considerably colder.

The door closed. I backed up to the little cupboard thing against the wall opposite the foot of Harris's bed and leaned my fanny up against it. I waved to Wendy through the narrow window.

Then I turned to Harris. "I suppose," I said, "that I should make allowances for your injuries."

"Especially my brain surgery, right."

"Bullshit. Your brain is as good as ever. I should have told them to stuff a little compassion in while they had you opened up."

Harris made his eyes round. "My, how upset. What have I done?"

"Well, for one thing, you continue to treat Shirley like a faithful puppy instead of as a woman who is seriously in love with you." He started to open his mouth. "Don't bother to say anything. You do it, and you know you do it, if for no other reason than I've told you repeatedly. Shirley is a big girl now, and if she can get along on patronizing compliments, God bless her.

"But," I said, "until that tape stops rolling tonight, Wendy Ichimi is Network business. You *know* the cops and the Network are walking on eggshells trying to keep that girl alive. How she's going to step out on that ice like a bug on a plate, knowing somebody has killed three people, one of whom might easily have been her. Was *supposed* to have been. And then you run this crap about everybody is the victim of a felony if he lives long enough and implying she wouldn't necessarily survive hers when it happens. As if she didn't already, with the DMSO-cyanide cocktail."

"Maybe," Harris said, "she didn't."

"Didn't what?" I took a look out the window. Wendy was smiling at Shirley, who was probably apologizing for Harris's rotten behavior. The Harris Brophys of this world always seem to find somebody like Shirley to apologize for them.

Harris said, "Maybe she didn't have a narrow escape from a murder attempt. I can't believe you haven't been thinking of this yourself. You're sentimental, but you're usually sharp, too."

"Thinking," I said, controlling myself, "of what?"

"Thinking that everybody who got murdered was supposed to be murdered?"

"What's that supposed to mean?"

"That the killer didn't make any mistakes, Matt."

"You mean," I said, intrigued in spite of my anger, "that Bea Dunney was the target all the time?"

"That's what I mean."

I shook my head. "The only way that could have happened would be if *Wendy* had done the poisoning herself."

Harris said nothing.

"No, Harris," I said. "It won't work. How could Wendy have known Bea was going to ask to borrow the DMSO?"

Harris tried to shrug, winced. "That could have been luck."

"Luck," I said.

"Killers get lucky. Because there could have been dozens of ways for

Wendy to have gotten that stuff on the Dunney girl. Could have spilled it on her, accidentally. Poured some in her shoes."

"Reaching Harris," I said.

"Just open your mind up and think about it, Boss." He knows I hate to be called Boss. "You saw how she reacted to my tasteless remark."

"She got sick," I said. "What do you expect when you remind her her Christmas box may be wood with brass handles?"

"She got sick," Harris conceded, "but was it because of that? Or did she suddenly get a queasy feeling I was on to her?"

"You're incredible," I said. "Have you tried this out on Shirley?"

"Of course not. Shirley's too nice to believe it. But look at it, Matt. That call that got Brother to open the door. Could she have known about Brother and his coke deal? She was practically living in the guy's pocket, of course she could have. Did she hate Dinkover and his wife?"

"Why'd she kill Bea Dunney?"

"That death put Wendy in the clear," Harris said. His voice was patient with me, as though he were afraid I was going to be difficult and say that might not have been reason enough. "If you need a reason, there's always that movie contract."

I was exasperated. "I won't," I said, "give you the reasons Bea was better suited to the movie than Wendy was. I'll just tell you that Wendy spotted them all for herself. And I will add that you're making her look bad only if I'm willing to postulate that she's a complete psycho."

Harris was no longer being patient. "Naturally, Matt," he said. "For God's sake, you've seen the bodies—I've just had what the newspapers tell me and what Shirley gets from people at the Network. But it's obvious that this killer is not sane."

"It's not possible," I told him. "I've been with her constantly for two days. I've been sleeping with her."

Harris looked disgusted. Then that passed, replaced by a look of sadness. "Matt, you must really have it bad for our little ice skater. If you were in your right mind, I wouldn't have to say this. I know you think I'm a selfish son of a bitch, and I guess I am, but you're a good boss, and I worry about you—who knows what kind of asshole they'd replace you with?"

"Go ahead and say it."

"This wouldn't be the first time a woman has made a fool of you."

I looked at him. God knew I couldn't argue with that. I made him promise not to tell Shirley, then I left, promising myself I'd fire him as soon as he was healthy again.

"What hath God wrought?"
—First message ever
transmitted via
electronic
medium

CHAPTER EIGHTEEN

Lieutenant Martin was showing me how he planned to deploy his personnel around the Garden when Shirley Arnstein gave me the bad news.

"The Great Low-Light Experiment is off, Matt," she said. She explained that having a few minutes with nothing to do (something she, as a workaholic, found intolerable) she'd gone up to the ad hoc control room on the mezzanine to see how things were going. She'd arrived in time to see disgusted techys power down the whole business.

"Some kind of glitch turned up in that new Japanese camera," Shirley explained. "They can't get the aspect ratio adjusted properly—they keep losing things off the edge of the screen."

"What are they going to do?" Wendy asked. She'd been relaxing in a chair while the lieutenant had briefed me. We'd kept our voices down, but so had Shirley, and now I knew that Wendy's hearing was no less acute than her stepmother's.

Her stepmother had shown up earlier, and there had been a big reconciliation between them. Mrs. Speir believed, or had talked herself into believing, that the whole business was dead, though she was shocked to think Carla could have done such a thing.

It was, I suppose, heartwarming, though my heart would have been more thoroughly warmed if Mrs. Speir hadn't given me an incredibly dirty look on the way out. I was still on the shit list for sleeping with her little Wendy.

I answered Wendy's question for her. "No problem; this has all been planned for. The Network will use the stuff that belongs to the Garden."

I could see some of the tension leave Wendy's face. Not all of it. Not the inevitable tension fear for one's life tends to afflict one with. But the tension of indecision, the fear that after deciding to be brave, that she might not have the chance to skate after all, and might have to go through the whole process again at some other time. Or (and I damned Harris Brophy for planting the thought), was it some other kind of relief she felt?

Lieutenant Martin said, "Miss Arnstein, I want to put you in the control room. Cobb tells me that the director is going to have one camera scanning the crowd at all times, to get reactions to Miss Ichimi's skating. I want you to keep watching the, the—what do you call that TV screen thing?"

"The monitor," I said.

"Right. The monitor for that camera. Look at it constantly, see if anyone looks suspicious."

Shirley took a handkerchief from her purse and began to polish her glasses, as though to be absolutely ready to do a good job for the lieutenant.

"How do I tell you if I do notice something?" she asked.

"You'll have a walkie-talkie. Everybody will. You Network people—you in the control room, St. John, Kolaski, and Smith on the mezzanine for surveillance, and my people, who'll be in flying squads at strategic places around the building. Everybody will be using the same frequency that Garden security uses, and they'll be keeping their eyes open, too. Any questions?"

Shirley shook her head, smiled at me. "Thanks for bringing me in on this, Matt," she said. She was only happy when she had an important job to do.

"Don't mention it," I said. I was happy to have Shirley's eyes, and her brain behind them, watching that monitor. It wouldn't have been the same if Harris had shared his suspicions of Wendy with her.

Lieutenant Martin went on. "Okay, Cobb. You're going to stay with Miss Ichimi, right?"

"I'll meet her as soon as she comes off the ice. I'll usher her on there in the first place."

"Good. Policewoman Constant will be with you, too. I want some-body armed with you, just in case. I've got Rivetz in charge of a squad of ten men. They'll string themselves out along the ice, just on the outside of the sidewalls. If anybody tries to get down there, they'll take care of it."

"Sounds good."

"It'll be all right," he said. He raised his voice. "Don't worry, Miss Ichimi, we've got you covered." Back to me. "Constant will be right outside the door here. Outside of Rivetz, she's my best man."

Knowing how hard that incorrigible male chauvinist had fought hav-ing a woman assigned to him, I was more impressed with Policewoman Constant than ever. It would also be practical, if Wendy had to go to any ladies' rooms.

The lieutenant left. Wendy started to take off her clothes.

"I guess I'd better get ready now."

"You've still got time," I said, then looked at my watch to confirm it. Seven twenty-seven. Right as usual.

"Everybody's in place?"

"The security people? Yeah, the lieutenant's had a chance to get to his own post by now." Lieutenant Martin had left himself in command of the largest of the flying squads—mezzanine level, center ice, on the Eighth Avenue side of the Garden, almost directly across the way from the Network's erstwhile control room. "Shirley's had time to get to the control room," I added.

"They've let the crowd in by now," Wendy said. Her voice was kind of wistful.

"They have," I said. "Doors were supposed to open at quarter to seven."

"Then I ought to get ready."

She was still undressing, down to underwear now. I'd seen a lot of her body over the last few days, and it occurred to me I could see it a lot more before I got tired of it. The same was true of her personality.

I decided not to tell her about Harris's suspicions, though I had planned to when I left the hospital. To hell with it. I'll tell her afterward, I thought.

If there was an afterward.

That was pretty morbid, I told myself in disgust. I have long since given up trying to control where my thoughts will take me, but there was no sense getting defeatist about it.

Time to change the subject. "How's your knee?"

She flexed it. "It hurts a little. But," she said, "I don't think I'll be using DMSO any more. The government is right. That stuff is bad for you."

She started to laugh. Not healthy laughter, but a hysterical shriek that seemed to ripple up her body and burst out like a prisoner. It went on too long. I started over to her, intending to shake her out of it.

Halfway there, though, the shrieks turned to sobs, and she sank into her chair with her face in her hands. I lifted her, held her until she stopped.

"Matt," she said, "I'm *afraid*."

"Who wouldn't be? You don't have to go through with this, you know."

"But the *police*. The *Network*."

"Screw them both. They don't count. You don't have to skate if you don't want to."

She thought about it, and for a second I thought she was going to call it off, and so did she. It took a conscious effort to restrain a sigh of relief.

Then she stopped and shook her head. "No," she said firmly. "I've got to do it. If I don't, I'm letting some maniac ruin my life the way Dinkover ruined my father's."

"Whatever you say, Champ."

She laughed again, but it was a wholesome sound this time.

"What's so funny?" I demanded.

"The Network paid a lot of money, but they're probably going to get a lousy performance. Two days, no practice. No warm up."

"You'll be fine."

She put her little hands against my chest and leaned back to look at my face. "I should get you to make love to me now," she said.

"I don't think that will be such a good idea."

"It may be my last chance."

"You just knock that stuff off right now, all right? We'll do it tonight. It's Christmas Eve. I've always wanted to make love to a World Champion on Christmas Eve."

"If I live."

"I told you to stop that. Is it a date?"

"Of course. Dope."

"That's better. What are you doing tomorrow?"

"I don't know. Max was going to take Helena and me out to dinner, but the next time I see him I'm going to tell him he's through, and I don't want to do that on Christmas, even to him."

"Okay. Come with me to my mother's house tomorrow. Helena, too, if you want her."

"Matt, I can't do that. There won't be enough—"

"There'll be enough. Have you ever seen a thirty-five-pound turkey?"

"Thirty-five *pounds?* They don't grow that big."

"The hell they don't. We happen to be a family that loves leftovers. There'll be enough."

"I'd love to, Matt." She sealed a bargain with a kiss.

There was a knock at the door. "Fifteen minutes, Miss Ichimi."

Wendy acknowledged and began to put on her beautiful white shiny skating dress. Soon, there was another knock on the door, and it was time to go. Wendy took a deep breath, smiled, kissed me again, and opened the door.

It was amazing how well she could walk on those rubber-covered skate blades. I noticed this as she scrampered back into the dressing room after we'd gotten about five steps away from the door.

It scared me to death, and it didn't do much good for the police-woman's health either. After about a half second of shock, I followed, but Wendy was coming back out again as I got there.

"We forgot your package," she said. "You've got to open it while I'm on the ice, and tell me how you like it when I get back. It'll give me something to think about."

"You could always think about your routine."

She shook her head. "Some skaters do, but I've got to let it flow, or I screw it up. Here." She handed me the package and started off again for the arena.

There was more excitement before we got there. Ivan Danov ran up to Wendy, shouting as usual. Where had she been? Why had she not been in touch with Danov? How could she expect to skate without practice? Why did Max Brother not talk to her on this occasion? Why—

He stopped because it's difficult to talk when you're looking in the mouth of a .38. Wendy and I hastened to reassure Policewoman Constant that Danov was okay.

"Have you seen Brother?" I asked the coach.

"Yes, we are sitting together in the special box. Miss Ichimi may no longer wish to consult us, who have helped her become famous and rich, but we still take an interest in her career. Her mother is also with us."

"Stepmother," Wendy said.

"Don't get huffy, Danov, Wendy has had a lot on her mind. She'll talk to you after Christmas."

"How kind of her."

"Ivan, come on, I have to skate." Wendy waved her arms gracefully, getting loose. She'd been stretching in the dressing room on and off for hours.

For the first and last time, I saw Ivan Danov with no trace of bombast whatever. He looked at Wendy the way a proud father would and said, "Yes, child. You must skate. And your coach must not delay you. We will talk after Christmas, and you will explain the things I do not understand?"

"Yes, Ivan. And thank you. Thank you for everything."

I thought Danov was going to cry as he turned and left. I thought it was interesting that three of the ace suspects in the original murder were all sitting together. And here we were, all together at a skating rink once again. Cozy. Well, at least they could keep an eye on each other.

I turned to Wendy and said, "I wish you wouldn't do that."

She'd had her eyes closed and was breathing deeply; my comment made them pop open. The previous act had finished (one I'd never seen before—the Ice-Travaganza had had to make a lot of changes over the last few days), and we stepped aside to let them get off. Garden employees went out to freshen the ice.

"Do what?" Wendy said.

"Keep delivering these valedictories. You're going to be *all right.*"

She went back to the breathing. "Don't talk to me now," she said. "I have to get ready."

The time got closer; the lights dimmed. Looking around the arena, I could see the red tally light of the live camera like a bloodshot eye. Somewhere in the dark, someone wanted to kill Wendy. Maybe.

The announcer went into his spiel. Her gold medal. Her world and national championships. How this was going to be a special twelve-minute performance taped by the Network for a big TV Special (the crowd cheered). It all concluded with, *"Miss Wendy Ichimi!"*

I'd been watching Wendy during the buildup. She'd been completely divorced from the surroundings; from the planet Earth, it seemed. When her name was called, she exploded onto the ice; as before, to the center circle for a quick bow, then into the routine.

Possibly her last routine, but I quickly reminded myself that we weren't going to be defeatist.

Wendy had neglected one very important thing when she'd told me to open my present while she was on the ice—I would have to take my eyes off her in order to do it. The skating may have been routine for her, but it was still magic to me.

As she had told me just before Bea Dunney had died, it's a whole different show at ice level, a low-perspective world of long leaps and showers of ice crystals. It was a good two minutes before I could take my eyes off her.

I told the policewoman I'd be stepping aside for a minute but would stay in her sight. Then I stepped over to a service light and skinned the paper off the package. Just before I did, though, a silly notion scurried across my mind—if Harris Brophy was right, this might well be a bomb.

It wasn't a bomb. It was a Bible.

I smiled as I saw it. The sarcastic little wretch. She'd said my mother would like it, and so she would. I'd show up at church in the morning carrying a brand-new Bible.

It was a really nice one, too, bound in black leather with "Salton's American Bible" debossed on it in gold, Salton being the publisher. A little band around it said it was intended to marry the poetry of the King James version with the clarity of the modern-English Bibles (a worthy aim if I ever heard one), presenting it all in the best of modern graphics in a comfortable size.

I took a look inside. My opinion of how well the folks at Salton had realized their literary ambitions would have to wait. There was no question about the graphics.

They were beautiful. Two colors of ink; the words of God were in red. A glimpse at the New Testament showed me Jesus' words were done the same way. The paper was thin, but strong and opaque. The main text of the Bible ran down the middle two columns of the page; explanatory notes ran concurrently in the outer two columns. There were color reproductions of famous religious paintings, two-color maps and graphs, and line drawings done in a bold, strong style.

And one more nice graphic touch. At the top of each page, next to the page number, there was a little symbol for the book of the Bible we happened to be in.

I wondered idly if Dr. Dinkover, with his work on religious symbolism, would have been upset about this. I decided he probably would have.

I looked at a few of them. The Book of Genesis was represented by a small rectangle, diagonally divided into light and dark. Exodus had a stylized rendition of the tablets of the Ten Commandments.

Naturally, I had to see what they'd chosen for the Book of Matthew. I turned to the first book of the New Testament, where I found they had used the simple little stick-figure of a man.

Something clicked in the back of my mind. No that's not right. Something grated, the way the ends of a broken bone grate as the doctor tries to get them set. It hurt about as much, too.

I'd come across this before in religious books and paintings. Matthew, represented by a man. There was a stone carving at the church I was going to go to tomorrow morning. Four figures. Each Gospel writer represented. Matthew by Man, of course I'd remember that, and . . . And *what?*

I forced shaking fingers to turn pages. Saint Matthew was a man. Saint Mark was a lion. Saint Luke was an ox.

And Saint John was an eagle.

"Turn out the lights, the party's over."
—Don Meredith, *NFL Monday
Night Football* (ABC)

CHAPTER NINETEEN

I let Al St. John's name trickle through my head, letting it bounce off the facts of the case like steel balls through a pachinko game. It never failed to tally. I hated it. I tried again. It fell through again. I could be wrong. But there was no time to be wrong. I had to go with it.

A noise from the crowd told me Wendy had just done something spectacular. I didn't even look. I had wasted too much time already. I had maybe eight minutes before he struck.

I grabbed hold of Policewoman Constant's arm. "Get on your radio," I told her. *"Al St. John* is the killer. Al St. John. Got that?"

She was surprised. "St. John? *Your* man."

"Yeah," I said bitterly, "my man. That means I'd better go try to stop him, doesn't it?" The policewoman was unhooking her radio from her belt. "Try to get Miss Ichimi off the ice," I told her.

I turned my back and headed away before I could hear her ask how.

I tried to make a mental schematic of the building as I sprinted up the stairs. Al was on the mezzanine, along with Kolaski, Smith, and Ragusa, the rest of my Special Projects crew. They had quartered the arena—Al had the northeast, or about a third of the way around from where I was now. When Wendy finished her number, with that incredible, drawn-out spin, he would have a perfect vantage point to shoot from. If he had a silenced weapon, he could get off four or five careful shots. And I'd put him there.

Seven minutes.

I still didn't want to believe it. But it answered so many things. How Dinkover knew Wendy was at the Network the other afternoon, before we'd chased him with laughter. How Dinkover had known about Max Brother's drug sale—Al had *told* him, that's all. He found it in the Network files.

It explained how the killer knew to have the doctored DMSO ready for the moment I'd let him get at Wendy—that was more Network information. And he knew *when* to have it ready because I called him on the phone and told him I was turning Wendy over to him.

I reached the mezzanine level and took a breath. Five and a half minutes. I began running down the corridor. Cops asked what I was doing—I told them to follow me. I wasted a half minute identifying myself before they took me seriously. One of them would stand and watch the station; the other would follow me.

He didn't run fast enough. I got so far ahead of him, sometimes the crowd inside would drown out the sound of his footsteps.

The steel balls bounced. It was easy to see (none to goddam soon, though) what happened. Al decides to kill Dinkover. He approaches him as a friend, offers to help put him together with Wendy. He proves his sincerity by tipping Dinkover to Wendy's being at the Network, then gives him blackmail ammunition against Max Brother and tells him he might see Wendy at the Blades Club late that night. Dinkover is a determined old man, he wants Wendy to do her bit for him, he goes along.

Al mugs Harris for his keys. He's never liked Harris too well anyway, so he really lets things loose with the wrench. I was breathing hard now, but I had to use some breath to laugh. This was beautiful. He's got Dinkover inside—now he has to get himself inside. Harris and I each have a key to the Blades Club. He goes for Harris's. Maybe he doesn't want to hurt me—Shirley told me he'd said I reminded him of his big brother.

But he has to make it *look* good. Al knew me. That was his big advantage. He knew me. I'd been teaching him since before I became head of Special Projects. He could be sure, once we knew about the murder, we'd look for a connection between it and Harris's mugging.

So Al, to make it look good, goes downtown and trashes Harris's apartment, overdoing it a little, so we'd get the point. Too eager. He takes the obviously valuable stuff, the stereo, coin collection, etc., but never tries to fence it. Why bother? We're convinced of the coincidence—that's enough.

Then he makes it uptown. He sees Dinkover slip inside, then uses his stolen key and joins him before the old man can meet any of the others. He gets close to Dinkover, who has no reason to be suspicious, and rips him open with the knife. Al takes off. Sometime later, Shirley has him beeped to come to the Network. He hadn't planned on this, but it's nice for him—he finds out everything immediately now. And he can calm his nerves by calling Hárris's apartment every five minutes to see if I've arrived. To see if I've bought the burglary. Too eager, Al, I thought. It wasn't anything that couldn't have waited.

But the old man, with his desperate, muddled dying thoughts, crawls across the ice. To the flag. To the eagle. To tell us who killed him. The old, brilliant brain has just composed ninety thousand words or so on religious symbolism. And so the man who had hated symbols, called them a lie, grabs for one as his last act. Pulling the flag into his body to tip the flagpole, he takes hold of the eagle. The symbol for Saint John.

I remembered how Al had taken things so humorously every time I mentioned that eagle, making ridiculous strings of possible applications. I'd even noticed how out of character it was for him to make jokes. But it worked. I got irritated with myself every time I found myself thinking seriously about the eagle and what it could mean. Paul Dinkover wasn't the only person who didn't like to get laughed at.

The corridor began to take on the elastic proportions of a nightmare. I kept running, thinking, but not getting anywhere. A summing up of the whole case. Except I had to get there, or Wendy wouldn't take any bows after this performance.

I ran on. I could hear my breath and footsteps, and the roar of the crowd, and the clatter of the policeman, following me like a conscience.

Why did he want Wendy dead? (Why did he want *Dinkover* dead, for God's sake?) I couldn't answer either. But after he switched Wendy's DMSO for the stuff mixed with poison (and it had to be Al who made the phone call to get Mrs. Dinkover to the agent's office so the list of suspects would be complete), he made his boldest move. He planned to tie off the case with the "suicide" of Carla Nelson Dinkover.

I had wondered why she would commit suicide before she knew Wendy had died. That objection didn't hold for Al. Carla Nelson Dinkover *had* to be dead before any news of Wendy's death could get out—it wouldn't do for his next victim to hear of the death and talk to the police before he could do anything about it.

Besides, he had no way of knowing that there'd be a delay before I pulled him in by that little beeper of his. I might have called him immediately. It didn't happen that way, but if it had, he wouldn't have had *time* to fix the widow up with a poisoned drink.

The DMSO misfired, and Al went from bold to brilliant. He *deliberately* outlined all the flaws in the phony suicide—the note on the word processor, choice of weapons, the timing, and the rest. Made it plain he didn't believe any of it. Because by then, he knew he'd killed poor Bea Dunney (and now *I* was calling her that, I realized) by mistake. There would be more attempts on Wendy, but who could suspect old Skeptical Al, Matt Cobb's pal? He had read my mind and been one step ahead of me all the way.

He'd even, by God, reminded me that I hadn't walked Spot. It was worth a try. He gave me a few moments to precede him down the street, then came up out of the subway and waited for me. If he'd managed to drown me in the snowbank, he could have gotten inside and done Wendy, too, and who would have tagged him for it? Hell, he probably would have been a pall bearer at my funeral.

That hadn't worked out, but what the hell, there was always tonight. His boss and friend, Gullible Matt, would always give him another chance at America's Skating Sweetheart.

"God damn it!" I yelled. Why? All those chances, all those deaths. Why?

I had reached my destination—through the door and down a short flight of steps. With any luck, a flying squad of cops should have gotten there first. Over two minutes left, too. I looked at my watch to confirm it.

I opened the door to the arena and looked down the short, steep flight of stairs that led to where Al was supposed to have been stationed. I let my breath go when I saw that Lieutenant Martin and about four uniformed cops were there.

I caught it again when I saw Al St. John wasn't.

It made sense. I'd been too busy watching my life flash before my eyes to notice it, but it made sense. Why should he stay out in the open where anyone of fourteen thousand Wendy Ichimi fans might see his gun and raise an alarm? Why shouldn't he go, for example, to the hockey press box, a nice, private, semi-enclosed area directly at center ice?

I mentioned this to the lieutenant. He said, "I've got a man stationed there."

"Call him," I said. "See if you get an answer."

The lieutenant raised his radio to his mouth, but he said "Jesus" before he hit the button to call his man. I didn't listen to hear if either of them answered. In less than a minute Wendy would go into her final spin. Making herself a damn near perfect target no matter where Al St. John was.

"He's not there," the lieutenant said. "Why I ever let you bring a goddam killer into this—"

"Why does she stay on the *ice?*" I said, but I knew. She was soaring, wrapped up in her genius. She was being real. In about forty seconds, unless I was totally wrong, she would be dead.

I had to do something, so I did. I ran among the crowd, stealing sodas. Hot dogs. Popcorn. I was not making myself popular, but I didn't care.

When I had an armful, I ran down to the rim of the mezzanine, losing my balance for a second. Falling over would have accomplished my purpose, actually, but I wanted to be around when Al St. John was brought in.

I righted myself, then gave a heave and threw the garbage out over the ice. Wendy happened to be down this end, and one of the brown shiny sheets of falling soda splashed across the arm and skirt of her white outfit. She fell down, then looked up with an angry, hurt look on her face.

"Get up, goddammit, *get up,*" I growled.

I watched in joy as she rose and sprinted for the exit, holding her wet arm to the side. A little geyser sprang up just behind her. One shot missed. I sent mental signals telling Wendy to speed up. I was booed by thousands, and I stood there and took it until I saw Wendy, at the other end of the ice, stroll into the protecting arms of Policewoman Constant. Then I took a bow.

"Should have thought of that sooner," I told the lieutenant.

"Yeah. Let's get you out of here. There hasn't ever been a white man lynched in New York that I know of, but right now, you look good to become the first."

The crowd cheered the police for taking me into custody. Over the cheer, we could hear the sound of his radio. It was the man from the press box—he'd just seen someone running from the sheltered area alongside the box. Left the police radio behind.

"He had a weapon, lieutenant," the voice squawked. "Target pistol with a scope."

"Figures," I said.

The lieutenant was doing the equivalent of calling all cars. Garden security people would seal the exits. Spectators were to be instructed to keep their seats. "I don't care," he barked at one point. "Tell them Wendy is going to skate again, that the drunk who screwed up the ice has been arrested."

The cops would move out in sweeps, carefully but thoroughly, trying to find the culprit.

Ten minutes passed—no luck. The Zamboni had been out; the ice looked beautiful, the crowd was getting nervous. Lieutenant Martin, who had taken over a refreshment stand for a command post, took a sip of steaming black coffee, made a face, and said, "You know, there must be ten thousand places to hide in this goddam building. Can you get out of here through sewer pipes or something?"

Nobody knew. Rivetz, who had joined us to report that Wendy was safe and well guarded, said, "How do we know he's just not sitting among the crowd somewhere? We may have to screen God knows how many thousands of people before we find the son of a bitch."

"Fourteen thousand," I said.

"Thanks, Cobb. That cheers me right up."

I turned to Lieutenant Martin. "Is it okay if I go talk to Arnstein?"

"Who?"

"Shirley Arnstein. My Network person in the control room."

"What do you want to see her for?"

"Network stuff. More bad publicity out of this. I want to talk to her about how we're going to handle it."

"Yeah, what the hell. Go talk to her, if she hasn't slit all the throats in the control room and set fire to the goddam place."

"I get the feeling I'm going to have you busting my chops over this for a long time."

"What do you think?"

"I think I probably deserve it."

"Yeah, but you look like you've got something else on your mind."

I didn't say anything.

"You scare me sometimes, Matty," the lieutenant said. "Keep your eyes open."

"I will."

"And yell if you hear or see anything. I got word back from the ice that the bastard is using Devastator bullets. The exploding kind."

"The ones the President was shot with."

"Yeah, but for him, they didn't go off." His tone implied he wasn't entirely sure how he felt about that. "You might not be so lucky."

"I'll be careful," I said. I left him fast, before he could read my mind any further.

I did have something on my mind. I had my fury, but that only kept me going. I was pretty sure I knew where Al St. John was. I could feel the vibrations through the knife he'd stuck in my back, in the Network's back. It wasn't going to be easy, fun, or especially safe getting him out of there, but I thought I saw a way to do it that would risk the fewest possible lives. One. Guess whose.

My famous time sense. My practically infallible, totally useless weird talent. Useless until now. I stuck my left hand in my pocket to keep me from looking at my watch, then headed for the Garden's TV control room. When I got there, I checked the time on my watch. Five minutes. My estimate had been correct. So far, so good.

I knocked on the door, and a cop let me in. Lieutenant Martin had told them I would be coming, which was nice of him. I told the cop I wanted to talk to Shirley, and he pointed to a corner of the room.

The technical crew were telling each other dirty jokes—a technician tells dirty jokes at every available opportunity, and this was Golden Time. They paid no attention to us, which was okay with me.

"Matt, what is going on? Why do I have to stay cooped up here? Isn't there something for me to do? Why are you searching for *Al?* Is the killer after him, too?"

She said it all in one breath, like one of those compound words in German. It took me a few seconds to sort it all out. When I finally did, and told her I'd explain later, I thought she was going to explode.

"There *is* something for you to do, though," I said, and her frustration turned to eagerness.

"What, Matt? The officer doesn't want anyone to leave." She dropped her voice. "He keeps asking me out, the creep."

"He looks perfectly okay to me," I said. "Anyway, you don't have to leave here to do what you have to do. Do you think you can get Romeo to let you use the phone?"

"Of course."

"Good. In exactly eight minutes, I want you to pick up the phone and call the Network."

"Who do I ask for?"

Bad habits surface when I'm tired. *"Whom,"* I said, then realized I was being silly. "Me," I said. "You ask for me. It's imperative you speak to me as soon as possible. Don't take no for an answer. Got that?"

"You promise you'll explain this later? And why you were so mad at Harris this afternoon?"

"Both. But this first. Eight minutes, okay?"

"Eight minutes."

I took a deep breath, then headed back upstairs. I didn't, however, return to Lieutenant Martin. Instead I went to the room the Network had taken over. The experimental control room. I stood outside, breathing deeply. Al had a key to this room, I'd given it to him myself.

It was okay to look at my watch now. Three minutes before Shirley did her thing. I tried to see if there was a light on in the room, but the seal was too tight, and nothing leaked past the crack in the door.

I tried to reassure myself. Al wanted to wait out the pursuit and escape. Even if he wanted me dead, he might not recognize me in the split second I planned to stay highlighted in the doorway.

Unless, of course, he planned to blast anything that came through. I had to hope he didn't. Devastator bullets, I thought, and shuddered.

I got my own key and slipped it quietly in the lock. I began to turn it, then stopped cold. I eased the key back, removed my watch, and put it in my pocket. All I needed was to show a luminous dial to make me a perfect target. I took one last look at it before I stowed it away.

I had a long two and a half minutes ahead of me.

I turned the key, opened the door wide enough to get in, then jumped into darkness. Complete darkness in the windowless room.

I thought I heard a rustling. It could have been my imagination. I stood motionless against the wall about two feet to the right of the door.

It was time for me to say something. I wondered how my voice was going to sound. I was amazed at how quiet I could be.

I said, "I know you're in here, Al," then dropped to the floor and rolled.

It hadn't been my imagination. The muzzle flash was like lightning, and there was a cough and a pop, and the wall I'd been standing in front of cracked open.

"You're too late, Matt. Wendy is dead. Your little blossom. I got her."

I froze over. Began to open my mouth to tell him he was nuts.

Lay there on the floor with my mouth open. He was nuts all right—he *had* to be nuts after the shit he'd pulled—but he wasn't stupid. He was trying to rattle me, trying to get me to speak. So he'd know where to fire.

I wanted him to know where to fire, but not just yet. Not for (I estimated) another minute and three quarters.

I could make out different shades of darkness now, furniture and equipment looming up as blacker shapes. I got my arms and knees under me and made a fast crawl toward a desk. It brought another bullet that exploded against the wall six inches above my behind. For the first time in my life, I blessed Sergeant Mike Polanski, my army DI. "Keep those butts down!" Yes, Sergeant. Thank you very much, Sergeant.

I felt better with something solid between me and the gun. All I had to do now was get my timing right. And not give myself away.

Al was talking. "I knew it was going to come down to this, Matt. Just like Freddie. Me and you, me and Freddie. Like always, just the two of us."

I wondered who Freddie was, but I wasn't about to ask.

"Don't think you're going to run me out of bullets, either," he said. He sounded as if he were on the verge of tears or laughter. Or both. "I've got plenty of ammunition. If anybody tries to join our little party, I'll shoot them in the doorway. This will be just the two of us. We'll sit here until we can't stand it any more, then one of us will make a move. Just remember—I'm the one with the gun."

He sent another shot across the room by way of punctuation, then was silent.

After a while, he said, "I did the important one. I got Dinkover. I won't get away with it, but I got him. And I burned his book and erased it from his computer. All gone. That's something, right, Matt?" Another pause. "It was you who threw that stuff on the ice, wasn't it, Matt? Good Lord, it couldn't have been anyone else."

I was trying not to listen to him. As he had pointed out, he was the one with the gun, and if I made any move too soon, I was meat.

"Why so shy, boss? You were always ready to talk to me before. Taught me everything I know."

That's right, you bastard, I thought, rub it in.

St. John fell silent. Everything fell silent. I could hear my heart beating, and the more I willed it to quiet down, the louder it got. I concentrated on the time.

Mistake. I'd never had to concentrate before. I tried to relax and take a guess. The guess told me it was time.

Moving slowly, I reached to my belt and unclipped my beeper. I lifted it to the level of the desk top and put it down there. Then I slipped off my shoes and raised myself to a crouch. I began to circle to the right. At any second I expected a gunshot, but none came. I made it in silence past the corner, then along the right-hand wall, about halfway down. There was no cover, so I crouched against the wall, holding my breath.

I might as well have been back in the snowbank, suffocating. I couldn't dare to let my breath go; I'd pant my last breath as soon as he heard me. I was thinking, Shirley, come on, Shirley, please. I could feel my muscles tense up, as if they planned a suicidal leap just to get it over.

Shirley, for God's sake—

Beep—beeep—beep . . .

In the silence, it sounded like a scream. Al St. John started to laugh. "The beeper! I told you to wear it, and you listened!" He snapped off three shots, still laughing.

The gun was pointed at a right angle from me, and the muzzle flash told me where he was. I'd never have a better chance. I drew in air and dove for him.

I knocked him to the carpet, and we rolled. He was strong, but I already knew that. I hit him, gouged him, kneed him, but I couldn't make him drop the gun. I had my left hand on his right wrist, trying to beat his hand against the floor.

I felt the wrist start to turn. I pushed against it, but it was no use. He was using his stronger hand against my weaker, and he had the strength of madness to work with. He kept laughing.

I could feel his hand turn. In a second the muzzle would be pointing straight at my face. There was only one thing I could do. Still holding the wrist, I dove to my right and rolled.

The plan was to pull him over on top of me, with the gun harmlessly out to the side. It didn't quite work. He pulled the trigger before I was through. I was looking in the direction of the gun when it went off. That close, the flash was blinding.

Al stopped laughing. Stopped moving, too. I gathered my legs and put my hands down in order to stand up. I felt something sticky. Blood. Again.

The only sound in the room was the beeper and my breathing. I stumbled back to the desk to turn the beeper off. I felt my legs go. Before I passed out, I thought I heard laughing again.

"We now return control of your television set to you."
—Vic Perrin, *The Outer Limits* (ABC)

CHAPTER TWENTY

"He's coming around, Lieutenant."

"Thanks, Doctor. Are you conscious, you goddam asshole?"

"Lieutenant!" Wendy's voice.

"Well, he deserves it. Taking on an armed man. Could have been killed. Damn near *was* killed. I ought to run him in for stupidity in the first degree."

"Merry Christmas, everybody," I croaked. "I'm in the hospital, I take it."

"Still making deductions," the lieutenant sneered. "What was I gonna tell your momma if you died, huh? Answer me that. Hell of a way to greet the neighbors Christmas morning. 'Merry Christmas, your fool son got himself killed.'"

"I can't see anything—am I blind?"

"You've got your eyes closed, Matt." Wendy was being very patient.

"Oh." I opened them, then squeezed them shut again as a big observation light burned into my brain.

"You're okay," the doctor said. "Seems you just fainted."

"Good thing, too," the lieutenant said. "Or else I would have kicked your stupid butt. I'm glad you opened that door before you lost it completely, or you would have starved to death before we could have found you."

I didn't remember doing that. "I fainted, huh?"

I opened my eyes again and squinted up at the doctor. He was a young black man. Handsome. Nice smile. "Don't go all macho on us, Mr. Cobb. Could have happened to anyone."

After a while they let me sit up, and after another while I began to feel human. I told Lieutenant Martin about the eagle and the Bible and anything else he hadn't had a chance to be brought up to date on. Wendy interrupted frequently for kisses.

"Yeah, well we figured the Brophy stuff for ourselves when we broke into St. John's apartment."

"He had the coin collection?"

"And the stereo. And everything else. In a closet, but not even hidden, otherwise."

"He never thought we'd suspect him."

The lieutenant snorted. "If it weren't for an old man with a flagpole and a young fool with a Bible, we never would have. You going to church today?"

"As a matter of fact, I am. What time is it?"

"I thought you always knew what time it is."

"Not after I faint. Humor me, all right?"

"One thirty A.M. You say some prayers thanking God for saving you tonight."

"I will," I said. "I'll thank Him for letting me redeem myself. I made it easy for Al all along—I kind of thought it was up to me to stop him. I had visions of you losing cop after cop as you tried to storm the room. So I handled things in a way that let me avoid having that on my conscience."

The lieutenant looked disgusted. "Don't try to bullshit me, Matty. You were pissed off at your pal, so you went for him yourself. You better pray God forgives you for that, too, 'cause I sure won't."

"While I'm at it, I'll pray we find out why a guy I worked with for three years all of a sudden became a homicidal maniac."

Wendy shot the lieutenant a significant look. I pretended not to notice it. Instead, I asked Wendy if she'd repeated her routine.

"Matt!" she said.

"Did you?"

"Yes."

"Were you good?"

"I wasn't paying attention, dummy. I was worried about you." She turned to Lieutenant Martin. "I have to know," she said.

"You were terrific. Matty can relax; the Network's going to have a great show."

"No-oo! I have to know why he wanted to kill me."

The lieutenant stopped bantering. "How you feeling, Matty?"

"Fine. Can I go home."

"If you want to. Like you to do me a favor first."

"What's that?"

"Talk to our perpetrator."

"He's *alive?*"

"Alive and here. Conscious sooner than you were."

"He shot himself in the *face* for Christ's sake."

"Yup. Doctor says he was lucky; I don't know how he's going to feel about it. They've got him upstairs, right next to your pal Brophy. He's been asking for you since he woke up. Won't talk to anybody else. Won't take medicine until he sees you. Doctors are going apeshit. Frying Nun, too. She's been swooping around him like a vulture, hoping to get a statement to make things neat and tidy."

"I'll talk to him," I said.

Upstairs, I was stopped in the hallway by Shirley Arnstein, back at Harris's side. "Came through again, Ace," I said. "Thanks."

"It wasn't hard. I had to agree to a date with the cop though. I can always break it."

Or not, I thought.

"Harris is asleep, but he told me to tell you he's sorry. That you'd know what it means."

"I know what it means."

Shirley shook her head. "It sure doesn't sound like Harris." She went back inside.

The Frying Nun gave me a dirty look as I went to the room they had Al in, but she refrained from talking. I wished her a blessed and peaceful Christmas; she looked as if she were chewing lemons, but she managed to wish me the same.

It was another dark room. At first, in the dim light, I had the unsettling impression that the figure in the bed was headless, until I realized it was only the bandages blending in with the pillowcase. A clear tube went into the bandages where you'd expect the nose to be. Doctors and nurses did things with machines and charts.

"Hello, Al," I said.

"Hello, Matt. That's Matt Cobb, isn't it?"

"It's me," I told him.

"Good." Something, maybe the tube in his face, made his voice gurgle. "Everybody else out. Let me talk to the man, then you can do whatever you please. Leave me."

A few seconds later, he said, "Are they gone?"

"They're gone."

"Good. Well, Matt, it's over. I'm kind of relieved."

"That's nice," I said. I got a little queasy watching his mouth move and make the bandage wiggle. They'd told me what was under there.

"What did you do to me?" he asked.

"You did it to yourself," I told him. "All of it."

"All right, be sanctimonious if you want to. What did I do?"

"You mean besides kill three people?"

"I mean to my *face*. Good Lord, Matt, you act like I'm some kind of monster or something."

"Yeah. It was my face you had in the snowbank."

"I'm sorry about that. Things started to get out of hand."

"Out of hand. Okay. Here's what you did to yourself. You absolutely destroyed both your eyeballs and the bones of your face above your upper lip. It's a miracle none of the bullet fragments made it to your brain. You might have some kind of face rebuilt, but you will never see again."

A noise came from him. I decided it was a chuckle.

"I got Dinkover, though. I got him for Freddie."

"Who's Freddie?"

"My brother, Matt. Dinkover killed him."

I had a flashback to the lunch I'd shared with Wendy, when she'd said the same thing, in the same tone of voice, about her father.

"Frederick St. John. Dinkover destroyed him. You may have heard of him under the name of John Free."

It was beginning to make sense. "The Landover Four," I said. "He was the one who—"

"The one who was killed in prison. His stomach cut open with a knife." The gurgle got faster. "Dinkover had to die for that, Matt, he deserved it. He was a killer nobody could touch. He talked them into joining the worst part of the 'movement,' into doing the crime; made them get themselves convicted so he'd have martyrs to point to, then he forgot all about them.

"I kept myself up on him. For years. Since before I came to the Network. I found out he'd done it before. To Wendy's father. Others. I waited, getting myself ready. When Wendy came to New York to do her show, I knew it was time.

"I went to him, told him I was Freddie's brother, told him I wanted to help. The egomaniac didn't question me for a second. I set him up at the Blades Club, with a ready-made set of suspects in a totally different case that would come to nothing.

"It should have worked. It would have. When I learned he'd gone for that eagle, I was sick. I looked it up. An eagle for Saint John the Evangelist, because he spread the word of God."

"That explains Dinkover. But why his wife? Why Bea Dunney?"

"Bea was a mistake. You know that. I was after Wendy."

"Oh. Excuse me." I remembered how shocked Al had been when I told him Bea was dead. How he kept making sure it was *Bea* who'd been killed. If I'd been paying attention, I might have tagged him then.

"That was Dinkover's fault, too," Al went on. "Even after I'd killed him, he was causing evil. I had to get Wendy because she was the one who put you on to the eagle business. Dinkover's dying message. It was obscure enough, but she knew right away it was the eagle and not the flag that was important. You told me she'd said her father and Dinkover used to discuss religious symbolism in front of her. She could remember at any minute. I couldn't have that."

"Of course not," I said. I damn near gurgled myself. It was all I could do to keep from going over there and wrapping that tube around his neck.

"I had to kill Mrs. Dinkover for the same reason. I had no love for her, but I could have let her live if it weren't for the *eagle*. She helped her husband with his books—that was common knowledge. She might put it together, too. Plus, she had custody of his manuscript. The secret had to be in there somewhere. I had to get to it; and I had to kill her to do it."

"Are you trying to lay the basis for an insanity plea, or what?" I demanded.

"What are you talking about?" He sounded hurt.

"What were you planning to do? Kill everybody who ever read a Bible? Studied religion? Read Freud or Jung or Dinkover? Burn a million books?"

"I was buying *time*, Matt. It would have all been wrapped up when Mrs. Dinkover died, except that Wendy was still alive, threatening me. I had to try again. I thought I could stay ahead of you. You trusted me, and I knew how you thought. You taught me everything I know."

"There's an old saying. I taught you everything you know, but I goddam well didn't teach you everything *I* know."

"I guess so," he said, then gurgled a sigh. "Dinkover. Dinkover. I didn't want to kill those women. It's his fault. It's funny."

"Hilarious," I said. "If I go now, will you cooperate with people?"

"Sure, Matt, but I meant it's funny strange. I guess I'm Dinkover's last victim."

I looked at him. I'd known, or thought I'd known, the mind behind those bandages for three years. Liked the man, worked with him. I felt like I wanted to lean up against something, to feel something real. I said, "Good-bye, Al," then ran to the corridor where I took huge gulps of sane air.

Doctors and nurses and law officers went in to replace me. Before he went inside, Lieutenant Martin gave Wendy and me permission to leave.

I put my arm around Wendy and we walked away. She waited until we were in the elevator before she spoke. "Why did he want to kill me, Matt?"

"Nothing personal. He was afraid you were going to catch on about the eagle business. He wanted to silence you before you did."

"Oh," Wendy said. "Matt, know something?"

"What?"

"I *still* don't understand that stuff too well."

"It was your subconscious he was worried about."

"It doesn't make a whole lot of sense, does it?"

"Only if you let yourself go crazy with hate."

"Is that a message meant for me?"

"I'm too tired to mean anything."

The elevator stopped. We crossed the lobby and stepped out into a cold, clear morning. The stars and the snow were shining with us in between.

I took Wendy's arm and we walked off to find a cab. "Are we still going to make love tonight?" she said.

"Oh, yes. And hear my sister sing at ten o'clock mass, and let my mother feed us turkey till we pass out. I need some normal human stuff very badly about now."

Wendy walked a little closer to me. "Merry Christmas, Matt," she said softly.

I saw a cab and waved for it. "Yeah," I said, "Merry Christmas."

About the Author

The Cincinnati *Post* has called William L. DeAndrea "the best American mystery writer to emerge in the '70s." His first novel about Network troubleshooter Matt Cobb, *Killed in the Ratings,* won him an Edgar Award from the Mystery Writers of America for best first mystery. His next book, *The Hog Murders,* won him another Edgar in the very next year. *Killed on the Ice,* the fourth Matt Cobb mystery, follows *Killed with a Passion* and *Killed in the Act,* all published by the Crime Club. He is the author of two other mystery novels, *The Lunatic Fringe* and *Five O'clock Lightning,* and was a contributor to the popular anthology *Murder Ink.* Mr. DeAndrea has a degree in broadcasting from Syracuse University. He is married to writer Orania Papazoglou. They live currently in Europe.